Danny and the Real Me

Heartlines

heartlines

Vicki Tyler

Danny and the Real Me

Pan Books

First published in the USA 1987 by Signet Vista, Nal Penguin Inc.
First published in Great Britain 1988 by
Pan Books Ltd, Cavaye Place, London SW10 9PG
9 8 7 6 5 4 3 2 1
© Riverview Press 1987
ISBN 0 330 30519 0
FIRST BRITISH PUBLICATION
Printed in Great Britain by
Richard Clay Ltd, Bungay, Suffolk

1

I KNOW I'll never love another boy like Danny ever again. When I first met him, it was like I was seeing a whole new world, because I'd never known anyone like him before. I felt like nobody could really see him—what he was really like inside, I mean—except for me. I felt that if I could make people see him the way he really was—the way I saw him—then maybe they'd see the real me too. Maybe there'd be a new me that would surprise people a little and make them take a second look.

The problem was I didn't know who the real me was when I first met Danny. I don't know, maybe I still don't. See, I've always had this problem. It seems like I never know whose side to be on. And in my school everybody's on one side or the other of just about everything. Except me. Like when we have debates in social studies class, I always think both sides are right in a way, but Mr. Trelinsky never lets me raise my hand for both sides. And when it comes to important stuff like whether kids should be allowed to wear strange clothes to school and dye their hair purple, forget it, I'm hopeless. I mean, in one way, I think they should because it's their hair and their life and their clothes, and why should anybody care, right? But in another way it makes me kind of mad that a few kids can get the whole school going over something that doesn't really seem worth it, you know?

The most important thing you need to know about me is pretty disgusting, so I'll get it over with right away. You see, I'm one of those "good" girls who never does anything wrong. I don't mean that I'm perfect or anything like that. I've just never caused any trouble. Not even a ripple. Getting mixed up with Danny was probably the first real mistake I ever made, the first important thing I ever did that my parents and my friends didn't like. Maybe that's why it was so hard to give him up, to admit I was wrong about him. I guess the reason Danny and I got together in the first place was that he didn't see me as a good girl the way everybody else did— not at first anyway. He just saw me as a girl. A girl he wanted to know. A girl who was maybe kind of special.

So this is really mostly about Danny, I guess. No, that's not right. It's really about both of us. It's about what happens when you try to love somebody who's not like you at all.

2

I MET Danny last summer at Sav-Mor, the discount store where we both worked. It was sort of an accident that we got to know each other at all, since I worked one of the cash registers out front and he worked back in the stockroom. Mandy and Laurie, the other two cashiers, knew boys who worked in the stockroom, but I wasn't like Mandy and Laurie. See, I was planning to go to college and they weren't. So that meant we were kind of in different worlds. It sounds snobby to say it, I know, but I can't help it. That's just the way it is.

You probably know what I mean about different worlds. It's like that in a lot of schools, I think. Kids from certain kinds of families are in all the college prep courses and working like crazy to get into the "right" colleges. And kids from other families are taking other kinds of courses or else just hanging out waiting for high school to be over and real life to start. And everybody knows who's who. And everybody stays on their own side. That's one of the things I mean about taking sides. What I can't stand, though, is that usually you can't help which side you're on. It doesn't make sense.

Anyway, I ended up keeping pretty much to myself at the store. I tried to talk to Mandy and

Laurie, but like I said, we didn't have much in common. I always felt like I had to hide part of myself when I was talking to them. And like they knew I was doing it.

We all knew that kids like me weren't supposed to be working at Sav-Mor. I was supposed to be a camp counselor or a lifeguard or a mother's helper, or a summer intern in one of my parents' offices—something you could put on a college application. That's what all of my friends were doing that summer. But I'd decided I wanted to find out what the "real" world was all about. And I was regretting it.

The night I met Danny, Mandy and Laurie's friend Angela had come into the store with her baby. I knew Angela by sight. She'd dropped out of school two years before when she got pregnant. Now she was eighteen and married. The thought that someone so close to my age could be married was very strange to me, and I tried hard not to stare at her, to see if it showed in her face. Mandy and Laurie didn't bother to introduce me, and as the three of them whispered and laughed, I felt like a little kid who had wandered into the room while the grownups were discussing something private. Luckily, there weren't very many customers that night, so the second it turned seven o'clock, I locked up my register and told Mandy and Laurie I was going to take my break. They didn't pay any attention.

I usually spent my dinner breaks sitting at the Sav-Mor lunch counter by myself, reading a book and thinking about all my friends who were working outside in the fresh air or on their way home from plush New York City offices. And there I was, in a depressing discount store, wearing a depressing orange smock, breathing the stale air, watching frazzled parents drag cranky kids around, and ringing up junky merchandise that looked even junkier under the harsh fluorescent lights.

My parents were right about this job, I thought that night at the lunch counter. I'd just eaten my usual hamburger and had a few minutes to spare before getting back to my register. I closed my eyes for a minute and pictured a bubbling little stream in the woods. When I did that, I could kind of escape from Sav-Mor for a while, even though the smells of grease and stale popcorn at the lunch counter kept pulling me back to reality. Sometimes when I concentrated real hard on that stream flowing through my mind, I felt real calm and peaceful. But it wasn't working too well that night. I kept thinking back to Angela and her baby, trying to imagine what it would feel like to be a mother, thinking how strange it was that Angela and I could live in the same small town and yet be in totally different worlds.

That was really bothering me that summer, the way people could be so different, so far apart. That's partly why I took the job at Sav-Mor, because I wanted to break away from "my side" a little, to be a little different from everybody else I knew, to be a little more like other people. But it wasn't working. I hadn't really been able to get to know anybody there. Maybe I hadn't really made an effort with Mandy and Laurie. But they sure hadn't tried very hard to get to know me either.

I took a sip of my drink and sighed, wishing I could go outside for just a minute. One of the most ridiculous things about working at Sav-Mor was that the cashiers weren't allowed to leave the store during breaks. We had to stay "on the premises" at all times, as Mr. Wiseman, the manager said. My mother is a lawyer, and I kept meaning to ask her if Sav-Mor was violating my constitutional rights. I had a fantasy about taking the case to the Supreme Court and being on TV. I mean, it's one thing when you're at school and they tell you where you have to be all the time, but on a job you're supposed to be treated like an adult, right? The manager at Sav-Mor treated us more like ten-year-olds. Except my own parents never treated me like that, not even when I was ten.

Actually, my parents were pretty great when I was ten. They still are, I guess. But sometimes I think they wish I could have stayed ten forever.

What was really getting to me was the way they were always so right about everything. It really bugged me the way they always seemed to know how things were going to turn out. Like no matter what I decided to do, they were already three steps ahead of me.

I finished my Coke, closed my eyes again, and tried one last time to will myself somewhere else. I pictured myself sitting on a big flat rock in the middle of the stream and dangling my feet in the cool, cool water. I was just getting really into the fantasy of it when someone tapped me on the shoulder, and I almost fell off my stool. Especially when I opened my eyes and saw the boy sitting next to me, staring at me with a big grin on his face. A boy with a purple streak on the left side of his blond hair and an earring in his left ear. He was wearing jeans and a tight black T-shirt. His muscles were bulging out of his tan arms. Not the gross kind of muscles like weight lifters get. Nice normal muscles like men have but most boys my age don't. I couldn't help staring at his arms.

"Hey, was that some kind of meditating or something that you were doing, or were you just having a sexy dream?"

I was so embarrassed I didn't know what to say. But I could feel myself grinning back at him, without wanting to or meaning to. He had one of those smiles that was "catching."

"Um, no," I said, trying to let him know that I knew he was just kidding, "I was just, you know, thinking."

"Yeah, probably about some guy, right?" he said, nodding his head and still grinning so that I could see a big dimple in his cheek. "I can tell that look."

I felt kind of warm all over my body when he said that. He wasn't right at all about what I'd been thinking, but somehow I got the feeling that he *could* see right through me if he wanted to, like he could see all my secret thoughts.

"Actually," I said, telling the truth because I couldn't think of a good lie, "I was thinking about how much I hate this job. This place," I said, looking around in disgust.

"Hey, tell me about it," he said, nodding again. He looked around for the waitress so he could place an order, but she was busy at the other end of the counter. "I been here for two years and it seems like my whole life."

He was talking to me. Like I was a normal person. Like he couldn't tell I didn't really belong there. Like he accepted me. It was such a relief after all those long nights of saying hardly anything to Mandy and Laurie that I couldn't help smiling a lot the whole time.

"You go to West Branch, don't you?" I said. I knew he did. I recognized him. I knew he was in the class ahead of me and was going to be a senior when school started and that he hung out with a bunch of guys who were supposed to be kind of wild, guys who hung around outside smoking in the parking lot before school started. Guys who took off in their cars as soon as they could get away from school. I never knew where they were going so fast in those cars, but I'd always imagined them as having secret lives at night, when they did all kinds of things that my friends and I couldn't even guess at. Usually, boys like that made me really nervous. But this boy seemed different somehow. Or maybe sitting next to him in the "real" world instead of in school made it easier for us to talk. I don't really know.

"Yeah," he was saying, "I go to West Branch. I work here full-time in the summer and after school the rest of the year. You go to West Branch?" he asked. "I never seen you there."

I nodded my head and smiled, trying to think of some way of explaining why he'd never noticed me before. I thought of saying, "That's because all my friends are boring preppy nerds and all your friends are criminals." But of course I didn't. The last thing I wanted to do was hurt his feelings by being too flip. Instead, I glanced at my watch, then slid quickly off the stool, taking my unfinished Coke with me.

"I gotta get back to my register," I said, smiling in relief that I was leaving before we had a chance to get started on the subject of school.

"Yeah, see you around," he said casually. Then he called out to the waitress, "Hey, Marge, how about a burger?"

Like I said, I was relieved that the conversation was over, but kind of disappointed too, at the last minute. As if I'd expected something more. Don't ask me what.

By the time I got back to my cash register, Angela was gone, thank goodness. I was feeling kind of excited. At last I'd made a friend. I could tell by the fluttery feeling in my stomach that I already hoped we'd be more that "just friends."

The last two hours before the store closed, usually the worst, went by pretty fast. I didn't even mind listening to Laurie complain about her boyfriend—at least not as much as I usually did.

Laurie was only about four-ten, which made her look like a little girl sometimes, especially in the orange smock that was way too big for her. She probably wore a size three or something and the smallest smock they made was a ten.

Maybe that's why she wore so much makeup, I thought, as I straightened up the candy and gum boxes in front of my register. Maybe she was afraid people would treat her like a little kid if she didn't. Even though it was almost the end of the summer, I still couldn't get over the fact that she showed up like that every day. It must have taken hours for her to get ready for work, I figured. I mean, I wore makeup too, but for work I usually just put on a little blush and some mascara. Nothing special. Of course, I wasn't meeting my boyfriend after work the way Laurie always was. That's what she was complaining about. Or pretending to.

"All he ever wants to do is go parking after work." she sighed. "And I don't feel like it."

I stifled a grin and stole a glance at Mandy, who was rolling her eyes.

"Sure you don't," she said to Laurie. "Want one of us to trade places with you?"

"Who's trading places?" Danny asked, suddenly appearing at my register with a package of batteries for me to ring up. Nobody else had any customers. Why had he picked my register?

"We're going to flip a coin to see which one of us gets to go parking with Tony tonight because Laurie's too tired," Mandy explained.

They both knew Danny, I could tell. Mandy was even flirting with him in an easy casual way I envied. I rang up his batteries, put them into a bag, and stapled the bag shut with the sales slip showing on the outside. I didn't say a word as I handed him the bag and his change.

"Well, I got a quarter right here," Danny said, picking one out of his change. "What do you say, Jenny, think you're up for it?"

The other girls looked as surprised as I felt. How did he know my name? I wondered. Then I remembered by name tag.

"Um, not really," I said, sounding much too serious. "My car's in the parking lot, and I have to go straight home tonight."

Everybody laughed, of course, including Danny. How could I have given such a nerdy answer to what was supposed to be a joke? It sounded like I had taken him seriously.

My cheeks were burning as I took the cash drawer out of my register and waited for someone from the office to come and pick it up. When I looked up, Danny was still standing there, still grinning at me. I couldn't tell if he was making fun of me or sort of asking me to forgive him. But I couldn't help smiling back— again.

"So long, slaves," he called as he walked out of the store.

The other girls laughed and said something back. I stood there feeling really uncomfortable and left as soon as I could.

The next day at work I half expected Danny to show up during my break again, but he didn't. I'd bought a copy of *Rock Video* magazine to read during my break, in case he came along. It had articles about all the latest rock groups, and I figured that would give us something to talk about. Most of the kids who looked like Danny were really into wild music and MTV and all that: I'm more the Lionel Richie type myself. Anyway, like I said, he didn't show up.

Why am I doing this? I thought as I ate my cheeseburger, flipping through the magazine and glancing up from time to time to see if Danny was around. Why do I care? If I'd been with my friends Amy and Tara, I never would have looked twice at a boy like Danny. And he never would have looked twice at me, I realized. He would have seen right away where I fit in—from my clothes and the way Tara and Amy and I talked together—and he would have walked away without really seeing me at all. And I wouldn't have seen him either. But the Sav-Mor was neutral territory, I guess, someplace where our paths crossed in a way that never would have happened at school.

Thinking about all this made me sigh out loud. I was disgusted with myself for making such a big deal out of nothing. Here's what happened, Jenny, a voice inside me said. A boy talked to you for two minutes. Period. So what? What's the big mystery?

This sounds crazy, but sometimes it's like there are two me's inside—one that gets all excited about stuff and another me that gets disgusted with the one who's always getting excited and tries to bring her back down to earth. Sometimes they start talking to each other inside me and I feel like I'm cracking up.

Anyway, Danny did not show up at the lunch counter again. I finished my burger and got back to my register just in time to hear Laurie talking to Mandy about Tony again. There was hardly anyone in the store that night, so they were huddled together leaning on the counter.

"I don't know," Laurie was saying. "I don't know if I should do it or not. I mean, I think I love Tony, but what if all he wants is *that*?"

From the way she said "that," I knew what she was talking about, and I couldn't help blushing. I made a noise so they'd know I was there, and they all looked up, smiled at each other with their eyes, and stopped talking.

"Guess I'll take my break now, okay?" Laurie said.

When she came back a half hour later, she was laughing. "Danny Ondich is *so* funny," she said to Mandy. "He was telling me all about what him and his friends did last Saturday night. . . ."

I didn't hear the rest. I was too busy listening to that voice inside me, the one that's always telling me how stupid I am to get excited about things. He only talked to you yesterday because you were the only girl there, Jenny, the voice said. You're not his type. Forget it.

I got all the troublemakers in my line that night—a man who insisted I'd made a mistake and made me go over every single item on his sales slip to prove I'd rung them up right, an old woman who started complaining to me about the prices in the store, as if I could do anything about it, and then a real loser of a guy about twenty who kept asking me when I got off from work and whether I needed a ride home. He wasn't really serious, I could tell. He just wanted to see if he could make me nervous, and it was working. He was laughing at me, I could tell, but I didn't know what to do about it, except keep my eyes on the register and not look at him. I heard him laugh as he walked away, and then I finally looked up. Into the eyes of Danny Ondich. I was so embarrassed.

He put a bag of Cheez Doodles and a big bottle of Coke down on the counter, and he stared at me the whole time I was ringing it up. I could feel his eyes on me, and when I looked up and asked him for the money, he didn't smile the way he usually did.

"Hey, you okay?" he asked. I could tell from his voice that he really couldn't tell whether I was or not, and he wanted to know.

"I'm okay," I said, putting his stuff in a bag and handing it to him, along with his change. "I just hate it when guys act like that. It makes me so mad I just want to punch them."

He looked kind of surprised when I said that. Then he smiled a little and looked behind him to see if there was anyone else in my line. There wasn't. Then he said, "Maybe that's why he does it. 'Cause he can tell it really gets to you. Maybe the way you act sort of encourages it, you know?"

I thought about what he'd said. Something didn't seem quite right about it, but I wasn't sure what. I shrugged. "Maybe," I said. It felt like kind of a personal thing and I didn't really want to talk about it with this guy I hardly knew. "Well, he's gone now, so it doesn't really matter, right?" I said, smiling at him and hoping he'd stop talking about it.

"Hey, you gotta be ready for these guys," he said, grinning. "They're all over the place, you know?"

I laughed. "Yeah, I know," I said as Danny headed out the door. Then I noticed the woman from the office standing next to my register, waiting for my cash drawer. I handed it over and went to punch out at the time clock, thinking about what had happened, and what Danny had said about it.

When I walked through the first set of doors at the front of the store, carrying my smock over my arm, I saw Danny standing there with his back turned to me. There were two sets of doors you had to go through to get in and out of the store. In between was a little space with a gum machine and a ride for kids. It was a good place to wait if you had a lot of packages or it was raining outside. One person could run out to the parking lot and bring the car around front, while the other waited inside.

Danny was standing there, waiting for someone, I guess. "Good night," I called as casually as I could as I walked through the second set of doors and outside.

"Hey, wait," he said, coming through the door after me. He stood there for a second, looking at me in my jeans and tank top, and I couldn't help blushing. I realized he'd never seen me in my real clothes before, only in my smock.

"Hi," he said.

"Hi," I said, and waited for what he'd say next.

"Um, I thought you might want someone to walk you to your car or something," he said. "I mean in case that jerk is hanging around or something."

"Oh . . . um, that's okay," I said. "I'm all right. Really."

"Hey, I'll just walk you to your car, okay?" His eyes were looking into mine, asking me to say it was all right.

"Okay, sure," I said, wishing I hadn't parked so far away that night.

The parking lot was pretty empty by that time. Most people had already gone home. Mandy's car was still there, though. I knew she and Laurie were still back in the rest room fixing their hair and their makeup. As usual, Laurie's boyfriend Tony was sitting in his car right in front of the store, so Laurie could run out of the store and jump right into the front seat next to him, and they could zoom away to some private place.

I suddenly realized that I'd been thinking so hard about Tony and Laurie that I hadn't said a word to Danny.

"Sorry I'm so quiet," I said, when we were almost to my car. "I get like that sometimes, especially after work. I hate it there so much that when I leave I sort of space out and get really quiet for a while, you know?" I laughed a little and looked at him to see if he knew what I meant.

He laughed too. "Yeah, I guess I'm kind of the opposite. When I get off work, I like to turn up the car radio real loud and try to find something exciting going on." He looked around the quiet parking lot and grinned. "But there's not much exciting going on around here, you know?"

I smiled to show him I understood. We were at my car by then, so I opened the door with the key and got in.

"Well, thanks," I said nervously, with my hand on the open door. "You didn't have to walk me, though, but thanks."

He shrugged and grinned. "No problem. See ya." Then he turned and started walking away. But after I closed the car door and rolled down the front window, he turned back and called, "Hey maybe we could do something after work sometime."

I just stared at him, not believing my ears. Before I could think of anything to say, he had turned around again, heading for his own car.

I couldn't help smiling all the way home. I even turned up the car radio pretty loud, wondering if Danny and I were listening to the same station. The voice inside me that thought I was overdoing it and that nothing was really happening with Danny tried to get through, but I didn't pay much attention to it. Somewhere deep down inside, I knew that something new was starting, something secret that nobody—not my parents or my friends or even the cashiers at Sav-Mor—would ever expect to happen. Danny Ondich liked me. And I liked him too.

3

I HEARD my parents rushing off to work the next morning, but I stayed in bed until they were gone. I know this sounds stupid, but I was afraid something might show, like how excited I was about Danny, I mean. And I wasn't ready to talk about it yet. Especially since the night before in the parking lot seemed kind of like a dream. The voice inside me was still saying that nothing much had happened, no matter how you looked at it, but I knew, just knew, that wasn't true. Something *had* happened, something I wasn't ready to share with my parents or anybody else.

Sometimes it's tough being an only kid because your parents *notice* you so much. When I was little, some of my friends with brothers and sisters thought I was really lucky for getting so much attention—so much stuff, so many special trips—and I guess I was lucky in a way. Now, though, I just wished my parents would ignore me once in a while. Just for a change, I wished I could be invisible and not have my parents looking as if they were always ready to take my temperature whenever my mood changed.

My parents both work in New York City. Dad is a managing editor at a photography magazine, and Mom is a lawyer in a big firm. Basically I like them all right, but like I said, they were starting to get on my nerves. That summer I only saw them early in the mornings—if I got up before they left—or at night after I got home from work, which was fine with me.

After they left for the train station, I got out of bed, got dressed, went downstairs, grabbed an orange, and sat on a lawn chair in the backyard to figure out what I wanted to do that day.

It was a weird summer, not like any summer I'd ever had before. My closest friend Amy was away as a counselor at the camp that she and I had gone to since we were in the third grade, the camp I could have been a counselor at if I'd wanted to. And my other friend, Tara, was working at her mother's office in New York. Every time I thought of Tara having to ride the train to New York every morning—with her mother yet—I didn't feel so bad about Sav-Mor.

Anyway, working nights left me pretty much on my own during the day. Usually, my mom had a few errands lined up for me to do—"Since you're around anyway, Jen, you can really make my life a lot easier if you don't mind," she always said—and I didn't mind really.

Otherwise, I had the whole day until four-thirty totally to myself. I slept in a lot and usually I spent part of the day at the town pool, where Jeffrey Baylor works as a lifeguard. I've known him ever since we were both in diapers (really). It was an okay summer, but kind of lonely, I had to admit. Especially without Amy around. I didn't see Tara much either, since I had to work nights and weekends.

Now there was Danny. What was going to happen with Danny? The feeling of excitement inside me started up again, and this time the little voice couldn't stop it. It was too much fun to think about what might happen with "us" before school started. I peeled and ate my orange, thinking about Danny and enjoying that feeling inside me. Then I leaned back in the lawn chair, closed by eyes, and lay there in the sun thinking about Danny some more.

At lunch time I ate a sandwich and some potato chips, then grabbed the list Mom had left on the refrigerator for me. I took the car and did the grocery shopping, then brought the groceries home and headed for the pool. I spent a few hours at the pool talking to Jeffrey and some other people I knew and then went home and got ready for work.

Usually, with Jeffrey and my other friends, I refer to Sav-Mor as "the prison," but suddenly it didn't seem like such a prison anymore. I took a long shower and put on my cutest top and my tightest jeans. Then I spent more time than usual doing my hair and my makeup.

As I was leaving the house I thought, What if Danny asks me out tonight? Should I leave a note for Mom in case I'm late? I threw down my smock, my car keys, and my purse on the kitchen table and rummaged around for a sheet of paper. I scribbled a note to Mom about how I might be going out after work with some of the other cashiers, but that I wouldn't be too late. I knew she'd wonder about that because I'd told her that Mandy and Laurie hardly ever talked to me. But it was the only thing I could think of. I could have said I was going out with Tara, I guess, but Tara and I never did that on weeknights, because she had to get up so early for her job, and besides, Tara might just happen to call that night or my mother might just happen to talk to her mother.

Of course I could have just told my parents the truth, that I might have a date, but I wasn't really sure whether I did or not. And even if I had been sure, I'm not so sure I'd have wanted to tell them about it. The truth was, I just didn't want my parents to know about Danny—not yet anyway. I wanted him to be my secret.

That night I made sure I took my break at exactly the same time I had the night I first met Danny. But he didn't show up. Part of me said so what, but another part was disappointed that he hadn't remembered the time and tried to meet me. Maybe I had just imagined that he wanted to go out with me. Or maybe he just couldn't get away from the stockroom.

I tried not to look too depressed when I got back to my register. I shouldn't have worried. Mandy and Laurie didn't even seem to notice I was there that night. It was the longest, loneliest night I'd ever worked at Sav-Mor. And that's saying something.

The store closed at ten, and at five minutes to ten, I started looking around for Danny. Maybe he'd at least come through my register that night. But he didn't. He went through Mandy's instead. I heard his voice, and out of the corner of my eye I watched her ring up his potato chips and Coke. They were both laughing, and Mandy was asking him all this stuff about his car, like they were old buddies or something.

A voice inside me that never believes anything good is going to happen was saying, "See? What did I tell you? There's nothing special about you. He just likes girls, that's all."

I couldn't help looking over at him the last second before he left Mandy's register and headed for the front doors. He looked at me too for a second, but he didn't smile or say anything. It was kind of a serious look. Then he left.

I suddenly felt like crying as I punched out at the time clock. I couldn't figure out why I was making such a big deal out of the whole thing with Danny, but it was like I couldn't stop myself. No matter what I told myself about it, my feelings kept taking over. That had never really happened to me before.

Then, as I walked up to the double doors, I saw something I hadn't dared to even imagine might happen. Danny was standing in between the doors again, waiting—for someone. I hesitated a second in front of the doors, suddenly feeling scared again. Of what? Then I walked through the doors.

Danny heard me coming through the doors and he turned around. "Hi," he said.

I smiled. "Hi."

"Want to go for a ride?" he asked.

I must have looked unsure, because he quickly added, "Don't worry. I'll bring you back here later to get your car. It'll be all right here." Then he smiled that smile that was asking me to please say yes. The smile I couldn't resist.

"Okay," I said, letting out a big sigh. It was nervousness, excitement, and relief that this was finally happening, all rolled up into one.

Danny's car was a shiny red Camaro with white sidewall tires and those hubcaps with the little spokes in the middle. I don't even care about cars, but I couldn't keep from breathing a soft "wow" when I saw it. That seemed to please Danny.

I wondered how he could afford a car like that. I mean, my parents buy me lots of things, but they could never afford a car like that. And every penny I earned that summer (almost) was going into the bank for college, so I couldn't buy myself much either. Never in a million years could I afford a shiny red Camaro. My family's Datsun was the only car I'd ever driven.

"Nice, huh?" Danny said proudly. "It's in my dad's name, but I make all the payments myself. That's the only reason I stay at this place," he added, jerking his head back in disgust at Sav-Mor. "Soon as I turn eighteen, I'm gonna get a *real* job or maybe I'll join the Army."

Danny sure didn't seem the type to be in the Army, but I didn't say anything.

When he opened the door, I saw the empty Cheez Doodle bag and the Coke bottle from the stuff he'd bought at my register the night before. Also the Sav-Mor bag with the sales slip from my register still attached. Some wadded-up napkins and an ashtray full of cigarette butts. And two empty beer cans.

Danny looked embarrassed. "Hey, wait, let me get rid of some of this junk," he said, filling up the Sav-Mor bag. "See, I usually wash the car and vacuum Saturday, so it really looks better than this on the weekends."

I looked around the parking lot nervously. I was worried that soon the other cashiers were going to come out and see me with Danny. It could take them only so long to comb their hair. I know it was chicken of me to worry about something like that. But I suddenly had a feeling that maybe Danny felt the same way. He seemed pretty nervous too.

"There," he said, stuffing the bag of garbage into the backseat. "Hop in."

"Thanks," I said, getting into the dark car and waiting for him to get in on the other side. This is really happening, I thought. It's really, really happening.

The first thing he did after starting the car was to light up a cigarette. The second thing he did was to turn on the radio. Loud rock music with a heavy, driving beat filled the car. I looked at the numbers on the channel display to see which station it might be, but I couldn't tell. The car was filling up with smoke too, but luckily Danny rolled his window down just then, and I opened mine too.

"This is the only decent station around," Danny yelled over the music. "From New York, naturally. It's FM, so I only pick it up at night."

I nodded and smiled to show that I understood. I didn't want to try to yell over the music. My parents listened to FM stations from New York too, but only the ones that played classical or jazz or folk. I don't listen to the radio much myself. I know all the hit records and hot groups and stuff, but I don't flip out about music the way some people do. Especially not loud strange music.

"I'm saving for a tape deck," Danny said apologetically, yelling over the music again. "Is this okay?" he added, meaning the music.

I said sure, but I wasn't really so sure about it. I didn't really like the music much, but Danny did, and it was part of him I wanted to know about. I was kind of hoping he'd turn it down soon so we could talk and stuff. But I couldn't say any of that. Not on a first date. If you could call it a date. I wasn't sure.

"Ready?" he said, grinning at me, and I could see how glad he was to be out of Sav-Mor and in his own car listening to his music—with me—and suddenly I felt glad too.

You won't believe this—or maybe if you've ever known a boy like Danny, you will—but we drove around West Branch for almost an hour, and we hardly said two words to each other, and Danny never once turned down the radio. It was weird. In some ways, it was like Danny didn't know I was there at all. Except once in a while he'd look over and smile or else he'd put his hand on mine for a while. Once he reached over and put his hand on my leg for a few minutes, and I got that scary, excited feeling I'd had the moment before I walked through the door at Sav-Mor. But then he took his hand away to make a turn, and I felt relaxed again. And a little disappointed. Sometimes I felt like we were really together, like he was really sharing something special with me. And sometimes I felt like we weren't together at all, like he was far, far away.

Anyway, after a while I realized we were headed back to the Sav-Mor parking lot, and I started having that strange combination of feelings again. Relieved. Disappointed. And a little excited about what might happen next.

He didn't turn down the music until he had pulled right up to my car. The lights were out in the parking lot by then, and it was pretty dark, except for the lights they leave on in Sav-Mor at night. I realized we were sort of "parking" in the way Laurie meant. We were "parking" in a parking lot. I smiled a little at the joke.

"Have fun?" Danny asked, giving me that look again, the one that always made me want to say yes.

"Uh-huh," I said softly, and I honestly didn't know whether it was the truth or not.

He looked around the deserted parking lot and laughed. "Hey, this place isn't so bad without all the people around, is it?"

I looked around too and then I looked at him. "I kind of like it. It's peaceful." And I knew that *was* the truth.

Danny put his arm around me then and gave me a kiss that was the most serious kiss I'd ever had up till then. It wasn't one of those "getting to know you" kisses. The ones that just mean, "Hey, I like you. I think you're nice." It said a lot more.

I looked out the window at my family's practical little Datsun and tried to remember that I was a practical, sensible person. A sensible girl who was going to go home and lie to her parents. I reached for the door handle and didn't say good night to Danny until I was safely out of the car. He watched me get into my car and start the engine. Then he peeled out of the parking lot and was gone.

I tried to find Danny's station on my car radio on the way home, but I couldn't do that and drive at the same time, so I gave up and turned the radio off. And started thinking. One good thing about Danny's music, I suddenly realized, was that you couldn't listen to it and think at the same time. Maybe that was why he liked it.

I glanced at the car radio: 11:07. I tried to imagine what I could tell my parents I'd been doing with the other cashiers for an hour. Having a pizza maybe? I tried to picture Mandy and Laurie and me sitting around a little table at Mama Rosa's, laughing our heads off and having a super time, but I couldn't do it. Suddenly, I knew I couldn't go through with it. The lie I mean.

The weird thing is I really could have told my parents the truth. They're not the type that freak out or anything. I mean I have rules and stuff I have to follow but they always try to be real "open-minded" about my friends and things like that. They probably learned that from a book. They have a whole shelf full of books they've read to find out how to be perfect parents. And they are.

The problem was I didn't want them to be understanding about Danny. I wanted there to be one thing in my life that they couldn't touch at all. So I decided to tell them I'd just been driving around for an hour. It was sort of the truth. It might worry them a little because they'd wonder whether something was wrong, but I'd explain that I'd planned to go out with the other cashiers because they'd asked me, but at the last minute I'd backed out and felt sort of like a heel, so I just drove around awhile to work off some of my feelings. It was a pretty good story, I decided. One they'd like. Because it sounded "sensible" and like I was trying to "cope" with my feelings. My mother is big on coping with your feelings.

Mom and Dad were watching the news when I came in. I looked at them and wondered if I could go through with it.

My parents look kind of young, I guess—for parents, that is. In a way, they almost look like twins, or the perfect couple. They've both got curly, sand-brown hair and faces that smile a lot. Dad's got a mustache, and some of my friends say he looks kind of sexy, but he's just my father to me.

Anyway, you can sort of imagine both of them being young once, but it's like that was in another life or something. When we visit my grandmother, my mom's mom, at Christmas, she likes to tell me stories about my mother, times she got in trouble and what her bad points were. We all laugh about it, including Mom. But she seems so far away from all that now, so, I don't know, safe. I mean, I know adults have problems, like bills and work and getting old and stuff like that, but at least everything's kind of already been decided in their lives, settled. At least they know what to expect. I bet they don't remember what it's like when nothing's been decided yet, and you've got so many chances to mess up your whole life.

"Hi, Jen," Mom said, looking up when the commercial came on and she noticed me just standing there. As soon as she saw me she switched on her "motherly" expression—curious, understanding—and I hadn't even said anything yet. "How'd it go?"

For a split second, I considered switching back to the story about going out with the other cashiers, but I knew the story about driving around by myself would be a lot easier to tell, so I went with it.

I fell into an armchair next to the couch where Mom and Dad were sitting. "I didn't go," I said, frowning and trying to look a little depressed, but not too depressed. "I couldn't go through with it, so I made some excuse at the last minute and backed out." I raised my eyebrows in pretended disgust. "I feel like such a jerk." That was the truth, of course, but not for the reason they thought.

"Well," Mom said in her most understanding voice, "it would have been difficult to pull off if you felt that uncomfortable, so I understand why you couldn't go through with it. But I hope you didn't offend the other girls."

I shrugged. "I think it's okay. I mean I don't think they really wanted me around anyway. I think they just felt they had to invite me along for once, but they're probably just as glad I didn't go."

Dad looked up from the TV when a commercial came on. "So where've you been, Jen? Out running wild, huh?" It was a kind of joke he made a lot. It wasn't mean or anything. Just the opposite really. It meant that they knew they didn't have to worry about me because I was so good and responsible and all that.

"Sure, Dad," I joked back, playing my usual part in the joke, but feeling irritated that the thought of me doing anything wrong was so far-fetched. "Almost got arrested too, but I got away. I'm a real speed demon in that Datsun, you know."

They both smiled. "What *did* you do, Jen?" Mom asked, looking concerned. "Is everything all right? Anything you want to talk about?"

Better than all right, Mom, and no, I don't want to talk about it, I thought, enjoying my secret. If only you knew.

But I tried to keep a serious expression on my face. "Oh, I just drove around awhile, you know, just thinking. All this social stuff, you know, the way people are so different, like me and the other people working at the store, gets to me sometimes."

I hadn't meant to add that last part. It was true, of course, and even helped to make my story more convincing, but it was tôo close to what was really going on inside me about Danny. Too close to the stuff I didn't want my parents to touch. It was a mistake.

Dad looked up, interested. This was the kind of thing he liked to make little speeches about sometimes, so I braced myself.

"Well, Jen," he said, "that's an important part of life, you know, learning to live and work with people who are different and might not have been so lucky in their lives as you have. Maybe this job at Sav-Mor isn't such a bad idea after all if it gives you some experience with people. All you can really do in a situation like that, I think, is try to understand those differences and not judge people."

"And see the similarities too," Mom added. "I think it's important to realize that deep down all people have the same needs to be respected and have opportunities in their lives."

Mom didn't know much about Laurie, I thought. The only opportunity Laurie wanted was the opportunity to marry Tony as soon as possible. I wondered how understanding Mom would be about that if I told her.

"I don't know about that, Susan," Dad was saying. "I think being able to respect the differences is the important point."

"True, that's important," Mom said, her eyes lighting up, "but being able to see through those differences to the things people share is even more important, I think."

I sighed and waited for a chance to excuse

myself and go to bed. When they got going like that, they could talk for hours. Other people's parents argued about taking out the garbage and stuff like that. Mine usually argued about what the point of what they were talking about was. And half the time they seemed to enjoy arguing. Weird.

Anyway, it bothered me that by trying to lie about it, I had actually tipped them off about some of what was going on inside me. Except that it had nothing to do with Mandy and Laurie like they thought. At least they didn't know about Danny yet. And I was more determined that ever to keep him a secret.

Part of me still felt like a jerk for lying to my parents. But another part felt justified, in a way. See, I felt like my parents had just proved to me that keeping Danny a secret was really the only way I could ever have my own private life at all.

4

THE NEXT day on my break, I was reading a magazine called *Musician* (it looked more serious than *Rock Video*), hoping to find out something about the kind of music Danny liked, when he walked up behind me and put his hands on my shoulders. I saw Marge, the waitress, look our way with interest, and I started to blush until it felt like my entire body was turning red.

"Hi," Danny said casually, sitting down on the stool next to me. I was kind of hoping he'd notice the magazine, but he didn't seem to.

"Hi," I said. It was always kind of a shock to see him in person because I spent so much time thinking about him, and the fantasy Danny and the real Danny weren't exactly alike.

"Doin' anything tomorrow night?" he said, just like that. I mean he didn't mention the night before or ask me how I was or any of the things I expected him to do.

"Not that I know of," I said, smiling at him and wondering if he noticed the dangly earrings I'd worn that day.

"Good," he said. "I got an idea for something to do. Want to come along?"

I hesitated for a second and then said, "Sure." Something told me I wasn't supposed to ask what the idea was. Like it was a test or something.

"Great," he said. "You working tomorrow?"

"Oh, that's right," I said, disappointed. "I told Laurie I'd work for her. But maybe I can get out of it." Not without making her hate me forever, I knew.

"Hey, no problem," he said, touching my hand. "I'm working too. We'll just go out after, okay?"

I nodded my head and watched him walk away. Just like that. Then I sat there and tried to imagine what I was going to say to my parents about this. "See, I have this date with this guy I don't want you to know about," I could tell them. "And I don't even know where we're going because he didn't tell me, and I have a feeling he doesn't want me to ask." Right, Jenny, the mean voice inside me said. They'll really go for that.

When I went back to my register, Mandy and Laurie smiled at me in a way that made me wonder whether they knew something. But I was probably just being paranoid, I decided. Danny wouldn't talk to them about me, would he? Besides, there wasn't really anything to talk about. Not yet anyway.

For the rest of the night, I thought about the problem of what to tell my parents. I couldn't go on telling them stories about the cashiers or about driving around all by myself. And I didn't want to drag Tara into it. So that left the truth. Or something close to the truth.

I could say that a guy from school had come into the store (that was true in a way) and wanted to go out with me after work. And we weren't sure what we were going to do because he hadn't been expecting to see me there in the first place and had to go check the movie schedule and stuff like that. I was pretty sure it would work.

They wouldn't like me going out so late, but they'd know it was unfair to say no, since I'd been working so hard all summer. After all, I had to have some social life. And summer was almost over anyway. I'd be safely back in school before long. Maybe they'd even extend my curfew from twelve-thirty till one for just that night. That wasn't too likely, but you never knew.

After I clocked out that night, I saw Danny waiting between the double doors again and I was so glad. So what if he hadn't made plans to meet me there? At least he was there.

Then I heard Mandy and Laurie coming up behind me, and I ducked inside the toothpaste aisle so they wouldn't see me. I waited till I heard them giggle good night to Danny, then I headed for the doors with a huge grin on my face.

The grin disappeared when I saw three guys headed for the outside door and Danny going out to meet them. He wasn't waiting for me at all. He was waiting for them. As they all lit up cigarettes outside I felt a little shock go through me. They were the kind of boys who made my stomach tighten up when I passed them, the kind who usually made noises or said something crude to every girl who went by. One of them, Mark Stefano, had made a study hall teacher cry last year. And the rest of them were just as bad. And Danny was one of them right now. But he wasn't, I knew. Not really.

I waited until they left and then walked out to my car. My hand was shaking a little as I put the key into the ignition. I checked my side and rearview mirrors just in case Danny came back, but he was really gone.

That night I had a dream that I walked past

Danny and his buddies, and they all started
laughing and calling me names. The worst part
was I didn't know whether Danny was turning
against me or whether he just didn't see me at
all.

The next morning I woke up with a stomachache. That hadn't happened to me since I was
in the fourth grade and had a teacher I hated
so much that I dreaded going to school every
day. But I wasn't dreading that night. I was
looking forward to it. So the stomachache didn't
make sense.

"I've got a date tonight," I told my mother as I
sliced tomatoes and cucumbers for a salad at
lunch time. "After work."

"That's nice. Who with?" she asked absent-
mindedly as she dumped about five different
kinds of beans into a big bowl for another salad.
My mother is very big on beans. Gross.

"Oh, a guy from school who works at Sav-
Mor," I said as casually as possible. "We're going
to the movies," I lied.

Mom looked a little surprised as she glanced
up from her beans. "Oh," she said, also sounding casual, "I thought you said you didn't know
anyone at Sav-Mor."

"I didn't, until a few days ago," I answered,
feeling a little edge creeping into my voice. "Then
I met this boy—Danny. What kind of dressing
do you want on this salad? Blue cheese?" I
asked hopefully.

"No, just a tiny bit of oil and vinegar; it's
healthier. We're cutting down on cholesterol for
your dear old dad's sake, remember. Danny
who?"

"Danny Ondich."

"Hm. I don't recognize the name. What's he like?"

"What does it matter, Mom?" I snapped. It just slipped out.

Mom looked me right in the eye. "I guess what you mean is that it's none of my business, and I'll accept that . . . for now at least. I hope it matters to you what he's like, though."

I sighed. "Of course it does. I'm sorry. I don't know why I got so excited about it."

"Go tell your father we need his help out here, okay?" Mom said, casual again, letting the subject drop.

Thanks, Mom, I thought as I left the room. I don't deserve it, but thanks anyway.

Over lunch I brought up the subject of my curfew, and my parents were pretty reasonable, I thought.

"Look, Jen," Dad said calmly, wiping his mouth with a napkin, "aim for twelve-thirty but *be here* between twelve-thirty and one. Got it?"

"Got it," I said happily. At least that much was settled. I decided I'd tell Danny twelve-thirty anyway, just to give us some leeway.

I hung around the house all day, not doing much of anything, until finally it was four o'clock, and I could take a shower and start getting ready for work.

It's hard picking out something that you can wear to work and on a "mystery date" too. I decided that black cropped pants and a lacy white summer top were safe for just about anything. Then I stuffed a blue oversized blazer into a tote bag in case it got cool. As I fluffed out my soft-permed hair, I realized that Danny and I didn't "match" at all. I was so obviously preppy, and he was so obviously not. Maybe I should get my hair cut really short and put a purple streak in it, I thought. But I couldn't help laughing at the idea. Finally, I put on my "lucky" dangly earrings and left for work.

My parents were cleaning out the garage together as I got into the car. "Have fun, honey," Mom called as I pulled out of the driveway.

I didn't see Danny at all that night, and part of me worried that I'd misunderstood and he wouldn't be waiting for me after all. I wanted to spend some time in the rest room to make sure I looked nice for him, but I knew there was no way I could outlast Mandy and Laurie, so I just made a quick check in the mirror and was ready to dash out front.

Before I could leave, though, Mandy looked over at me and said, "Wow, Jenny, what a top!" Then she grinned. "Got a date?"

I smiled back nervously. "Yeah," I said. "He's waiting outside for me. Gotta go. Bye."

As I went through the door I heard Laurie call after me, "We want to hear all about it on Monday, Jenny. *Everything!*" Then she and Mandy giggled.

Oh great, I thought, but I didn't have time to worry about that.

I was so excited when I met Danny out front! I could tell by the way he looked at me when he first saw me that Mandy had been right about the lacy white top. It felt fantastic to have a boy look at me that way.

It was kind of exciting to wonder about where we were going too. Until I saw signs for the George Washington Bridge, that is.

"Where are we going?" I asked, turning to face Danny in the dark car and shouting over the loud music on the radio.

"To the city," he shouted back, grabbing my hand. "Surprised?"

"New York?" I said weakly. I'd only been into New York at night a few times before. Once to go ice skating at Rockefeller Center and see the giant Christmas tree there. And another time to see the Broadway show, *A Chorus Line.* Both times had been with my parents.

"Oh, but . . ." I started to say that my parents would have a fit if I went into New York without telling them. But I knew what Danny's answer would be to that. We didn't have to tell them. They'd never have to know.

"But what?" he said, turning to me in the darkness as we waited in line to pay the bridge toll. It sounded kind of like a challenge, and I didn't understand why he was talking to me like that.

"Well . . . I have to be home by twelve-thirty. I know it's dumb, but I do."

"Twelve-thirty. Come on! You gotta be kidding," he said. "Are your parents living in a time warp or something? Don't they know what decade this is?"

I just shrugged my shoulders helplessly.

He paid the toll and accelerated the car to about sixty miles an hour in five seconds. That seemed to make him feel better.

"Okay," he said, "that gives us two-and-a-half hours. Forty-five minutes in. Forty-five minutes out. That leaves us an hour. It stinks, but I guess your parents don't leave us much choice, right?" He looked over at me. "Hey, we're not going to let them ruin tonight, are we? Don't worry. I'll get you home on time, okay?"

When he saw that I was still worried, he got angry. "I said don't worry, all right?" he repeated.

"All right," I said, wishing I meant it. I wanted to say that we did have a choice, that we could have just stayed right in West Branch, but I was afraid that might make him angrier.

"Hey," he said, turning up the radio, "it's Saturday night. Let's party and forget all this heavy stuff, okay?"

"Okay," I said again, smiling this time and trying to get into the music, wishing I really could forget all the heavy stuff. When Danny put his hand on my leg and started stroking it to the music, it was a little easier.

Danny really knew his way around New York. He was driving us through parts of the city I'd never even seen before. I didn't know exactly where I was, but I knew it was pretty far away from the ice skaters at Rockefeller Center. I was worried about how the date was turning out, but I couldn't help being excited at the same time. It's hard not to feel excited when you're sitting in a dark car with a cute guy with the radio blasting and all around you the lights and people of New York are whizzing by. All kinds of people going all kinds of places. Rich people and poor people. Black, white, and Chinese people. Beautiful girls with all the latest new wave hair and clothes. Crippled old people hobbling across the street. Drunks and bag ladies sitting in doorways all by themselves. Groups of laughing kids on their way to some adventure. It was hard to imagine that in a few minutes I'd be out of the car and part of the whole scene and somebody might go by and wonder about me the way I was wondering about the people I saw.

As we waited for a light to change Danny looked over at me and smiled. "How ya doin?" he asked.

"Great," I said, meaning it.

"Sure beats downtown West Branch, right?"

I looked around me for a while and thought about what was happening on Main Street in West Branch right then. The only places open would be the pizza parlor and Baskin Robbins. And the only people you'd be likely to see would be the ones getting in and out of their cars. And they'd probably be people who lived in houses a lot like yours and wore clothes a lot like yours or your parents'.

"Yeah, it sure does," I said.

"The Village, this part of New York, is my favorite. There's so much going on and all kinds of people doing it, you know? This is where *Rocky Horror Show* started, you know?"

"Really?"

"Yeah, me and my buddies came in to see it when we were in eighth grade. It was unreal, all the costumes kids were wearing and stuff."

I'd never seen the *Rocky Horror Show*, but I'd heard a lot about it. Mostly, I'd read about it in magazines. But Danny had actually done it and a long time ago too, back when I was still going to all-girl birthday parties.

"Danny, can I ask you something?"

"Yeah?"

"Where are we going?"

He was grinning, loving every minute of the suspense. "Well, I'll give you a hint. Soon as I get us into this parking space, we're almost there," he said, squeezing the Camaro into a space about half the size of the car.

Next thing I knew, we were on the sidewalk.

Danny took my hand as we walked through the crowded streets. The sidewalks were so packed with people that sometimes we couldn't even walk side by side. But he just pushed ahead and pulled me after him. We were passing all kinds of tiny little boutiques and restaurants and record stores and T-shirt shops and movie theaters. I had no idea where we were or where we were going.

For a while I just watched all the people swirling by. Lots of them were kids our age, hanging out and lounging against the parked cars along the street. They were wearing some of the strangest outfits I'd ever seen. Some of them made Madonna seem boring. There were outrageous combinations of lace and leather and leopard skin, or neon-green shirts, black stretch pants, and orange-striped socks. Hair that was pink, deep red, bright yellow, or green and cut short and sculpted into strange shapes.

In West Branch some kids looked like that—Danny did—but they really stood out. On this street, I realized, I was the one who stood out because I was wearing such a perfectly matched outfit. A white lacy top with a black blazer and black pants. Gold dangly earrings, pink socks, and white flats. I was the one who was a freak.

Danny must have read my mind because a few seconds later he stopped in front of a blanket that was spread out on the sidewalk. Displayed all over the blanket were wild neon jewelry and sunglasses. A man was sitting next to the blanket saying, "Check it out, two dollars each. Check it out, only two dollars," over and over.

Danny pulled out some money and bought me some orange neon bracelets and leopard-striped sunglasses.

"I can't wear these now," I complained as he put the glasses on me. "It's dark out."

"They look good," Danny said proudly. "They make you look older. Anyway, don't worry. Just hang on to me."

"Where are we going?" I finally asked after a few more blocks.

"You'll see," he called over his shoulder. "We're almost there."

The buildings were getting shabbier now, and there were more drunks and homeless people on the streets. I had heard a lot about bad things that could happen to people in New York, and this looked like one of the places where they could happen. Finally, we turned down a street that was almost totally deserted, and I got really nervous. Then we turned another corner, and Danny pulled me into the entryway of a building that was closed for the night. "Okay," he said, "now all you have to do is be cool and act real mature. We're going across the street to the hottest rock club in the whole city, where all the top groups play. We're underage, of course, but I've gotten in before. Just look like you couldn't care less, you know? Real cool, like you do this every day."

How was I supposed to look cool in my perfectly matched shopping-mall outfit? How was I supposed to act mature when I felt like I was about five years old compared to everybody else around me?

Danny opened the door of a huge crumbling old building, and we walked into a small area that looked like the box office of a theater. We—I mean Danny—had to pay a lot of money for tickets, just like for a play, before we could go in. This was the hottest rock club in the city?

Instead of being cool, like I was supposed to be, I sort of cringed behind Danny, trying to be invisible. I'd taken off my blazer, hoping I'd look sexier and older with the lacy top showing. So far, though, nobody was paying much attention to me.

Danny grabbed the tickets, pulled me along, and when he opened another door, there was an explosion of loud rock music, flashing lights, video images projected on huge overhead screens, and wildly dancing bodies dressed in costumes like the ones I'd seen on the street. If Danny hadn't been pulling me by the hand, I probably would have just stood there unable to move, hypnotized by all the overpowering sensations.

"Isn't this wild?" he yelled over the music as a waitress led us to a table. He looked even happier than he had when we were listening to the radio in his car after work, so I smiled encouragingly, even though, once again, I couldn't really tell whether I was having a good time or not. I mean, it was kind of exciting in a way, but I felt too tense and keyed up to enjoy it.

Then a waiter came over to our table and was about to take our order for drinks—"order a beer," Danny had whispered. "I'll drink it if you don't want it"—when he took a good look at me and shook his head.

"Hey, man," he said to Danny, loud enough so everyone around us could hear, "who is this, your little sister? Give me a break and get out of here, all right? I can't afford to lose my license."

I gave Danny a panicked look, but he didn't even flinch. "Hey, man," he insisted, "she's twenty-two. Back off and bring us some beers."

"Sure she is," the man said, pulling our table away from the wall so we could slide out. "Get out of here, okay? Show's over. Time for you two kiddies to be in bed."

My cheeks were burning hot, and Danny looked mad enough to start a fight. This time I was the one pulling on him, trying to get him out of there.

"Come *on*, Danny. I want to go home." It was already eleven-thirty anyway, I suddenly discovered, glancing at my watch. It was just as well we'd gotten thrown out. We barely had time to walk back to the car and get home in time for my curfew as it was.

Out on the sidewalk, Danny shook his hand away from mine and started yelling at me in front of all the people who were streaming by. "Want to go home now, Jenny? Is that what you want?" he said, sounding disgusted. "I'm not holding you hostage, you know."

Was he so angry at me? It wasn't my fault we'd gotten thrown out. It wasn't my fault I was only sixteen and looked my age. He should have know better than to take me there. It was a stupid idea in the first place. I didn't say any of that, though. I didn't say anything. I just stood there staring at the sidewalk, wishing I could just sink right into it and disappear.

"Let's go then," Danny said, rushing down the sidewalk ahead of me. This time he wasn't pulling me by the hand. He looked more like he was running away from me.

"Wait a minute!" I shouted after him. "Shouldn't you get your money back?" But he didn't even turn around. I had to run to keep up with him, and I had a feeling that if I couldn't he'd just keep on going without me.

Now the car is going to break down, and I'm going to have to call my parents and ask them to pick me up and it's going to be all over, I thought. They'll stop being so understanding when they find out I've lied to them. They'll never let me see Danny again. That is, if I was even going to see Danny again.

But that's not what happened. We got in the car, and Danny drove me back to the Sav-Mor lot to get my car. Danny was speeding, but we didn't have an accident or anything. I knew I should tell him to slow down, but part of me just didn't care.

He didn't say a word or even play the radio. He hated me now, I was sure. I'd ruined the date, ruined his surprise, that's probably what he thought. He didn't even seem to care about the money we'd wasted, even though he'd spent about half a week's pay that night.

When we got to the deserted parking lot, Danny didn't kiss me or anything when we said good night. The dash board clock said 12:25 when I started up my car.

Pull yourself together Jenny, I told myself, trying desperately to think of something to tell my parents when I got home.

5

I KNEW it was all over as soon as I saw my parents sitting there on the couch watching a movie.

My mother looked up as soon as I came in. Her expression was cheerful and full of curiosity about my date. "How'd it go, Jen?" she called.

I looked at her and couldn't think of anything to say. Not one single thing. I felt the tears coming and I tried to run upstairs before they could see.

Mom knocked on my door a few minutes later. "Jen," she said softly, "can we talk?"

When I didn't say anything, she walked in and sat down on my bed. "Jenny, what's wrong?" she said, stroking my shoulder. "You know you can tell me."

I looked up at her and then started crying again. She waited, not saying a word. Finally, I managed to get a few words out. "I . . . I . . . lied to you. About my date with Danny. We didn't go to the movies at all."

Mom looked hurt, like I knew she would be. "But why, Jen? Why did you feel like you had to lie to us?" she said. Haven't we always—"

"Yes," I sighed, interrupting her. "You've always been great. I know that. It's just that . . ." I hesitated, still not able to tell the whole truth, about how I needed my own private life. So I said, "I couldn't tell you the truth about where we were going because I didn't know myself. Danny wouldn't tell me. And I wouldn't tell you what Danny was like because . . . I don't know, maybe I wasn't so sure about him myself. I guess that's why."

Which was partly true, I suddenly realized. No matter what I thought about Danny seemed to be true, even things that seemed totally opposite.

Mom nodded and said very softly, "So what happened, Jen? Why all the tears?"

I sniffed and wiped my eyes with a tissue, then sighed. "It wasn't anything bad, really. It's just that I let Danny talk me into going into New York with him. And he took me to this bar and stuff and I knew we could get into real trouble because we're underage, but I kept going along with it, until finally we got thrown out and I asked him to take me home and he did. That's all." I saw the worried look still on her face and I added, "Really, Mom, that's it. I'm just . . . disappointed, I guess."

She nodded and smiled sadly. "I'm sorry you couldn't talk to me sooner, Jen. I hate to think I'm the kind of mother . . . well, never mind."

She was quiet for a minute, then smiled again. "I guess everybody has to learn some things the hard way, but we parents always think we can spare our children that somehow."

"What did you ever have to learn the hard way?" I asked, and it came out sounding more like a challenge than I'd meant it to.

Mom noticed that and gave me a curious, surprised look. "Well," she said, biting her lip as she thought about it. I tried to imagine what

wild things from her past she might be remembering and deciding not to tell me about.

"Well," she said again, "I guess I tended to fall
for guys who were kind of on the wild side."
She had a big smile on her face all of a sudden.

"Dad?" I said skeptically.

Now she laughed out loud. "Hey, we weren't
always as boring as we are now. And he wasn't
the first guy I went out with, you know. I got
around a little. Anyway, one thing I learned the
hard way was how to speak up for myself and
not let the boy make all the decisions. Like you
did tonight. It sounds like you've already figured out that this boy isn't for you, and maybe
you learned something about speaking up for
yourself when you're with boys and knowing
what you want and don't want in a boyfriend.
That's all important." Then she smiled again
and said, "And you're all right. That's what
really counts. Anything else you want to talk
about?"

I shook my head no and she kissed me on the
forehead, said good night, and left.

My mother had just done it again, I thought.
She had a way of making all my messy problems sound like they boiled down to a few simple "lessons" I had to learn. I could never make
her see that it wasn't that simple. Especially not
when it came to Danny.

The next day, Sunday, I was off from work,
and Tara and I went swimming at the town
pool, the one where our friend Jeffrey was
lifeguard.

"Look at me," Tara said, stretching out in
her hot-pink bikini. We had just come out of
the water and laid down our towels by the side

of the pool. "I'm so pale it's absolutely gross," she continued. "That's what I get for working in an office all summer. It's so hot and crowded in the city that I don't even feel like going out at lunch time. But my mom keeps telling me the experience will be worth it. I hope so. Lucky you, you can come here every day if you want to. You've got a great tan this year."

I shrugged and lay down and closed my eyes, trying to feel peaceful inside and not think about Danny, even though I hadn't thought about much else since the night before.

"I guess so," I said at last, finally replying to Tara's comment that I was lucky.

"I can't believe this!" Tara said in amazement, and I opened my eyes to see what she was talking about. She had propped herself up on one elbow and was staring down at me.

"What?" I said.

"I just said how lucky you were to be working at Sav-Mor, and you didn't even make your usual joke about how hideous it is. What's wrong with you?"

I tried to laugh it off. "I guess I'm just running out of jokes about it," I said. "Besides, I'll only be there two more weeks. Then we'll all be back in school, and I won't have to worry about it anymore."

"Yeah, I guess you're right," Tara said. "For me, it's going to be hard going back to school, though, after being treated like a real person all summer. But I'm really excited about cheerleading. And scared stiff. Tell me I'll be all right."

I sighed. "You know you will be, Tara. You're terrific."

Tara went on talking about how nervous she was about cheerleading and about other school stuff that she wanted to get involved in this year. I felt about a million miles away from her. It wasn't that I didn't want to tell her about Danny. It seemed like it was *impossible* to tell her. Everything that had happened with him suddenly seemed so unreal. And the thought of going back to school seemed pretty unreal too.

And when Jeffrey came over and started talking to us, I got even more confused. Usually, he's one of my favorite people. He's smart and funny and always seems so sure of himself, but not in an obnoxious way. But that day he just got on my nerves because he seemed so perfect. And so boring. I suddenly missed Danny so bad.

When Jeffrey asked Tara and me if we wanted to go to a movie with him when he got off work, I was glad I had to be home for an early dinner and couldn't go.

I felt kind of lonely as Tara drove me home that day. But it was almost a sweet kind of loneliness, like it was somehow something I wanted. Maybe spending so much time by myself that summer had made me kind of different from other people, I decided. Maybe I was becoming some kind of a freak. But I just didn't care.

The next morning I slept in till eleven o'clock and dragged myself around the house feeling really depressed. When the doorbell rang at noon, I figured it was the mailman with a package or something. He usually came about that time. But it wasn't the mailman. It was Danny.

"Hi," he said when I opened the door.

I just stood there in my shorts and T-shirt and bare feet, stunned. "Hi," I finally said.

Then he just stood there, staring at the ground instead of looking at me. When he finally looked up, he said, "So I just wanted to talk. About Saturday."

"Oh, okay," I said, feeling excited and hopeful and scared all over again. "Um . . . let's go out back, okay? I was just going to have a Coke. Want something to drink?"

Danny didn't answer right away. He was looking around the house, taking it all in, and I tried real hard to see it through his eyes.

Our house is really old, but kind of cute in a way. It's a big wooden two-story house, painted white, with a huge front porch and a nice private backyard. My parents bought it a long time ago, right after I was born. Before that, they lived in New York, which is kind of hard to imagine. Dad says they bought this house because it was incredibly cheap and two blocks from the train station. But Mom says they "fell in love with it" as soon as they saw it. I can believe it about my mom. She's always "falling in love" with things, especially old things.

There were old things all over our house. Old quilts and Indian blankets hung on the walls like pictures, an old-fashioned braided rug in front of an old-fashioned couch, old-fashioned patchwork pillows and lots of plants and books. The only modern thing around was my father's sound system, which I wasn't allowed to touch. And the kitchen, of course, which had a microwave and food processors and all that junk.

"My parents are kind of old-fashioned," I apologized to Danny.

"Yeah, this looks kind of like my grandmother's house, except for the stuff on the walls," he said, looking puzzled by everything.

"Do you want something to drink?" I asked again as I popped the tab on a can of Coke for myself.

"Yeah, how about a beer?" he answered in that challenging voice he sometimes got.

"Um, sure," I said, reaching in the fridge for a bottle of the imported beer my parents drank and wondering if I knew where to go in town to replace it so my parents wouldn't ask about it. And whether the store would sell it to me. "Is this okay?" I said, holding it up.

"Sure," he said, smiling at me. Even his smile seemed to be a challenge that day.

We went to sit out in the backyard, but even there my parents had left reminders of who we were all over the place. A beautiful flagstone path. A pretty white wire-mesh table and chair set with a big yellow beach umbrella over it. My mother's perfect rose bushes. For the first time, I saw how perfect it *all* was, the whole house, and I was embarrassed.

Danny and I didn't say anything for what seemed like a long time. I sat curled up in one of the chairs smiling nervously, and Danny sat across the table from me, peeling the wet label off the bottle of beer. When he did start talking, I forgot everything I'd said to my mother about him being all wrong for me.

He cleared his throat. "I came over to say I was sorry . . . about Saturday . . . but I'm not, not really." He was staring ahead at a point just to the right of my face, but then he shifted his gaze right into my eyes. "See, I thought you'd really like it in New York. I thought maybe you and me . . . had something, you know, in common. I wanted to show you something that was . . . special, you know?" He looked around at the yard and the house and laughed. "Pretty stupid, huh?"

"It's not stupid," I whispered. "It *was* special in a way. It's just that . . ."

"You think I'm a real jerk," Danny finished the sentence for me.

"No I don't!" I insisted. It was weird. Even though I thought Danny *had* acted like a jerk part of the time on Saturday, when he said it, I felt like I had to deny it, to protect him or something. Like I couldn't let him put himself down.

"You don't," he said with a little smile.

"No, I think you're . . . really interesting," I said. "I think most people, you know, they kind of go along doing all the things people expect them to do. But you and me . . . I think we're different in a way."

He looked at me for what seemed like a long time but was probably only a minute. It felt like a minute that would last forever. It didn't last forever, though, because the neighborhood bees were starting to swarm around my Coke, and finally Danny and I had to go inside.

We sat down on the couch and he reached out and pulled me over to him. I cuddled up next to him with my head on his chest and it felt so peaceful. So private, so special, so real. Then Danny started running his hand up and down my leg, and I knew by the way he looked at me that I had to ask him to leave right away because I wasn't ready for what that look meant. Just two nights ago, I hadn't ever wanted to see him again. I was so mixed up. I jumped up off the couch and said, "Gee, I forgot, I have to do some errands for my mom before work. Want to come along?"

He laughed. "Sounds exciting, but I gotta go."
Then he walked right up to me and ran his
hands down my arms. I felt a chill that didn't
come from the air conditioning. Then he put
his hands on my face and gave me a kiss that
was long and slow.

"See you tonight, okay?" he said cheerfully as
he left.

I stood there for a long time after he left.
Danny was so changeable. One minute he could
be angry and then he'd be real intense and
affectionate and then he could just be real casual again. Just like that. It was confusing but
exciting.

Sorry, Mom, I thought, half afraid and half
glad about what I was thinking, it's not so
simple as you thought. You don't know everything there is to know after all. Not about Danny
Ondich anyway.

6

THAT'S WHEN my secret life with Danny really started. That night after work, we sat in his car in the Sav-Mor parking lot listening to the radio for a while. Danny always parked in the farthest, darkest corner of the lot, which meant that we could sit and watch everyone leaving Sav-Mor, but no one could see us inside Danny's dark car. It was a wonderful, private feeling. After a few minutes, everyone was gone, and the parking-lot lights went out.

"Want to go for a ride?" Danny said, reaching for the stick shift.

I hesitated. "I don't know," I finally admitted. "I mean, I don't know whether I should."

Danny shook his head in disgust. "Hey, nobody's forcing you to be here, you know. You want to go or not?"

"Well . . . see . . . I sort of told my parents I wasn't going out with you anymore."

"So?"

'So, if I come home later than usual, they'll wonder where I was."

Danny shrugged. "So, lie. Make something up."

I sighed. "I can't. I mean, it wouldn't work," I explained, realizing I'd be willing to do it if I thought it would work. "See, they know I don't

58

really have any friends at the store and my real
friends are away for the summer or have to get
up early to go to jobs in New York. And they
know I wouldn't go out by myself, and I couldn't
make up another boy, that would be too hard,
so . . ."

Danny gave me a hard look. "Hey, Jenny, give
me a break, okay?" he said. "Make up your
mind. Stay or go. I want to get out of here."

I felt like he hadn't heard a word I'd said.
Why was he acting like that? Couldn't he tell
that I really wanted to be with him? Didn't he
care? He was just sitting there with his hands
on the steering wheel, and he was staring
straight out the window.

I tried to get him at least to look at me. By
then I was almost in tears. "Danny, please . . ."
I started, but he interrupted me by leaning
across me and opening the car door on my
side.

"Hey, just go home, all right?" Danny said,
still not looking at me. "I'll see you tomorrow."

"But . . ." He was starting the car and still
staring straight ahead, so I got out real quick
and slammed the car door. The tires squealed
as he made a sharp turn out of the parking lot.

I stood there alone in the dark lot trying not
to cry, wondering what I'd done wrong this
time. I could have stood there a long time like
that except it was kind of scary. I'd heard of
girls being attacked in parking lots before. Besides, if I didn't hurry home soon, I'd have to
explain to my parents where I'd been anyway.

Everything had been so great at my house
that afternoon, I thought on the way home.
What happened? Being with Danny was kind of
like being on a roller coaster. One minute I'd be

really up and the next minute I'd come crashing down.

When Danny showed up at my house the next day around lunch time, I was a little surprised but very, very happy. When the doorbell rang, I was sitting out back in my bathing suit working on my tan. I threw on one of my father's old shirts that I like to wear around the house and ran to the front door.

"Hi," Danny said, smiling at me as if nothing had happened. He looked me up and down. "Hey, what are you wearing?" he said, softly grinning at me.

I laughed. "Don't worry. I've got my bathing suit on underneath this," I said.

"Hey, I wasn't worried," he said, still grinning and looking around the house.

A few seconds passed while I tried to decide what to do next. I had turned up the air conditioning in the house and I was shivering a little in my bathing suit. That and the fact that Danny and I were alone in the house together again made it hard for me to think.

"Want to have lunch?" I finally said. "I was just going to make myself a burger."

"Sure," he said casually, falling into my father's chair and putting his feet up on the coffee table.

He watched me the whole time I made the lunch and didn't offer to help once, which bugged me, I have to admit. When the burgers were cooked, I put them on paper plates with some potato chips and handed Danny his, saying, "Let's take these outside, okay?"

As I was doing that, the phone rang. It was my mother. Sometimes she called home during the day with a list of things to do that she hadn't gotten around to putting on the fridge. She had lists for everything.

"Hi, Mom," I said, trying to sound normal while Danny stood there grinning at me. "Wait a minute, I'll get a pencil." I rummaged around nervously in the kitchen looking for something to write with. I was half afraid Danny would pick up the phone or something just to shock my mother, but he didn't. "Okay," I said, back on the phone. I wrote down *dry cleaning, salad stuff,* and *ice cream.* Mom thanked me a million for helping out and then asked me what I was doing. I hesitated for a split second before I said, "I'm just having my lunch. I better go. My burger's getting cold."

"Okay, honey," Mom said. "See you tonight. Don't work too hard."

"You too. Bye."

I'd done it. I felt like a traitor or a spy. Keeping Danny a secret made me feel kind of guilty but it gave me kind of a thrill too because I'd never had a secret life before.

"You know, you're really weird," Danny said, laughing at me as we ate our burgers out in the backyard. "I mean what's the big deal? Everyone lies to their parents, right?"

"Do they?" I said, wondering if he was right and feeling really stupid for not knowing.

He shook his head in disbelief again. "I can't believe you," he said. "You're too much sometimes."

"Is that good?" I said in a teasing voice, but really wanting to know.

But he didn't answer. Instead, he crushed his paper plate and stood up. "Want to go for a ride?" he said, repeating the question from last night and making it sound like a challenge.

"Well, I have to . . ."

"*Do* you or don't you?" he said insistently.

I hated the way he was always putting me on the spot, but I did want to go, so I said, "Sure. Just let me change and get my mother's list. Could we stop at a few places?"

He shrugged. "Who cares?" He looked me over again. "Why do you have to change?" he said, challenging me again. "You look good like that."

I laughed nervously. "Because nobody goes grocery shopping in a bathing suit, that's why," I insisted.

"So why do you have to be like everybody else?" he said. "Why can't you just be like you?"

I thought about that and tried to imagine myself walking through the Grand Union in my bathing suit. I couldn't. Not even with the shirt over it. Not even to prove something to Danny. "I'll be right back," I said, rushing upstairs to change. "It'll only take a minute to put some shorts on."

I slipped on a pair of shorts and came back still wearing my bikini top with the big shirt over it, but Danny didn't seem to consider that very daring.

It was a lot of fun riding around town in Danny's car with the radio blasting and all the windows down. He kept the motor running while I ran into the dry cleaner's, and he stepped on the gas as soon as I got back into the car, before I even had a chance to lay the dry cleaning across the backseat.

"Hey, slow down a minute," I complained as the dry cleaning bag flapped in the wind.

We both laughed as I struggled with the flapping plastic bag and finally dropped it into the back.

Danny went inside the grocery store with me, and I rushed through it hoping I wouldn't run into anyone my family knew and have to introduce Danny to them.

"Hey," Danny said, rubbing his hand up and down my back after he'd kissed me good-bye at my house, "let's go swimming tomorrow. I want to see more of you in that suit."

I blushed but couldn't say no. It was so exciting to have secret plans.

That's how Danny and I spent the last two weeks of the summer, making secret plans. We'd sit in his car in the dark after work every night and maybe drive around for a while making plans for the next day. And the next day he'd come over and we'd sit on the couch for a while kissing and doing other stuff until I got kind of nervous and suggested we get going. I was curious about sex, sure, and I knew some girls who "did it" with their boyfriends, but I wasn't sure I was ready for that. Something inside me still held back, like I wasn't ready to deal with all that yet. I sure didn't want to take a chance on getting pregnant, I knew that much. And the thought of going to the birth control clinic was pretty embarrassing. But when Danny touched me the way he touched me when we were on the couch and looked at me the way he looked at me then, it was hard to think about all that practical stuff. The only solution I could ever come up with was to get us both out of there.

"What is it, babe?" Danny whispered when I got up from the couch.

"Let's go out Danny, okay?" I asked him. "I'm worried about my parents coming home. We could go to New York for the day," I added, trying to appeal to Danny's sense of adventure and restlessness.

"Guess you don't trust me alone, right Jen? Gotta have millions of people to keep Danny Ondich in line," he laughed.

I laughed too. It was true. I was only safe with Danny out in public, that was becoming clear.

"So, whatta you want to do in the big, bad city, little girl? You pick this time," Danny told me. I guess he didn't want a rerun of our last experience in New York.

I knew right away what I wanted to do.

"Let's go to Central Park and walk through the zoo and get hot dogs and popcorn," I suggested. My parents used to take me there as a kid, and I thought it would be fun—and totally different—to do all that kids' stuff with a boyfriend.

"If you say so," he said with a shrug.

I could tell it didn't sound very exciting to him, but he went along with it anyway.

"I've got to stop by my house and get some money for gas and stuff, okay?" he said next.

"Sure," I answered, wondering about two things. What was his house going to be like? And was he just making an excuse to get me someplace quiet where I wouldn't worry about my parents coming in?

As we drove over I realized I would get to find out a little more about Danny. I already knew a few things—that both his parents worked, that he had a younger brother and sister. But getting Danny to talk about anything personal was something I hadn't figured out how to do yet. Usually he mumbled answers that didn't even sound like a yes or a no, and after a few minutes of one-sided conversation like that, he would usually turn up the radio in the car.

"I've been hoping to go over to your house," I said as we drove along.

"Why? It's just a house."

"I'd like to meet your family sometime," I ventured.

"Yeah," Danny answered without much enthusiasm for the idea. "Hey, it's just you and me, Jenny," he said, reaching for my hand.

Danny had a way of silencing me with his touch, his smile, and his special looks. He made all my attempts at small talk seem unimportant, as if we didn't need words to communicate. It just took getting used to, that's all.

Danny's house was in a new development, where there wasn't a tree or a bush higher than a couple feet. All the houses looked alike, mostly split levels that looked as if they'd blow down in a strong wind.

"Here it is," Danny said as he screeched into the driveway of a house that looked as if it was still under construction. There was a pickup truck in the driveway and a couple of bikes that seemed to be rusting on the patchy lawn.

We went inside. Though no one was home, the television was blaring. Everything was pretty dim, since no one had bothered to raise the shades.

"Want to see my room?" Danny asked.

"Only if I can stand in the doorway," I joked, trying to keep things light.

"Follow me," Danny said, leading me down a hallway that was littered with toys.

I'd never been in a boy's bedroom before, so I was a little nervous, but when I saw Danny's room, I couldn't help smiling. He shared a room with his little brother. One side of the room was covered with G.I. Joe figures and baseball equipment, while Danny's side was almost bare, with just one poster of a sexy girl and a shelf with a few trophies on it.

"I didn't know you played sports," I said in surprise as he rummaged through his drawer, looking for extra cash.

"Oh, that was back in junior high," he said, making it sound like it had happened to someone else. "I was pretty good in basketball."

"Why did you quit?" I asked.

"It's not worth it. All that training crap and being pushed around by the coach and stuff. If you're gonna get treated like that, you might as well be in the Army where it really counts for something. Let's go."

On the way to the city, I had to ask Danny something I'd been wondering about. "Did you really mean that, about joining the Army? Remember, the night we first went out, you said you might do that?"

"Sure, I might," he said, keeping his eyes on the road. "So what?"

"But why?" I said. "I mean somebody like you, the way you look and the things you like to do . . . I mean the Army's so different. All the rules and stuff? Why would you do that?"

"Because it might be worth it, not like the basketball team, that's why. You put in your time and you end up with something. You know, they train you in like electronics or computers, so you can make good money when you get out."

I thought about that for a minute. "You know that commercial they have on TV, the one with the song that goes, 'Be all that you can be'?" I said. "Well, my mother says the person who wrote that song should be arrested. She says it's all a lie and they just want warm bodies to send to war."

Danny took his eyes off the road for a second when I said that, and when he turned to me I realized I'd made a mistake. "Yeah, well, your mother's full of shit," he said angrily.

We didn't talk anymore all the way to the city, and my feelings about Danny changed that day. Till then I'd thought of him as being exciting and more grown-up, more experienced than me. But now I felt older than him in some ways, like I knew some things he didn't, like I had to protect him in some way. Even though he looked so strong on the outside, I decided, there was a part of him on the inside that wasn't so tough or sure of himself at all.

When we got to the city, I tried to be real gentle and nice, to make up for hurting his feelings. He pulled away from me at first, but it was such a gorgeous day that he couldn't stay in a bad mood for long. We fed the animals in the zoo and then explored the park until we found a bench in a private spot and sat down.

Danny was staring at some squirrels nearby, still kind of far away. Suddenly I put my arms around him and gave him a big kiss, which was pretty daring, for me. "I'll never mention my mother again, I swear," I said afterward, holding up my right hand like I was taking an oath in court.

"Good," he said. "Come here." He pulled me into his lap and we sat like that for a few minutes until an old couple came along walking their dog and we decided to move on.

You never really know someone until you see where they live, I decided on the way home.

*   *   *

The night before school started, I was finishing up my last shift at Sav-Mor when Amy and Tara burst into the store. Before I saw them, I heard them coming—to be exact, I heard Amy squeal my name.

"Jen-ny!" she screamed, running up to me and almost jumping over the counter in excitement. "I made it home at last! Can you believe it!" Then she giggled and looked around at Mandy and Laurie, who were already raising their eyebrows and looking at each other as if to say, "What is this?"

Amy looked great. Her short dark permed hair had grown out a little, and she had a super tan. As soon as I heard her familiar nervous giggle, I realized I hadn't thought about her in weeks. And that I missed her.

"Hi, Jen, working hard?" Tara said, walking calmly up to the counter in white shorts, a purple tank top, and a hot-pink scarf tied into her blonde wavy hair.

Tara looked perfect, I thought for the one millionth time in my life. Some people are jealous of their beautiful friends, and of course sometimes (a lot of times) I wish I could look like Tara. Mostly, though, when it's just the three of us—Amy, Tara, and me—I kind of forget how perfect she is. When we're around guys, I get embarrassed at the way they react to her. And when we're around other girls who don't know Tara, I get apologetic. I keep wanting to tell them to give her a chance and not hate her immediately just because she's beautiful. With Mandy and Laurie, though, I could tell it wouldn't have done any good. I could tell. They hated Tara as soon as they laid eyes on her.

"Hi, guys," I said nervously, suddenly feeling more ridiculous in my Save-Mor smock than I'd felt all summer. "What's up?"

Amy looked a little hurt, like she'd expected me to make a bigger deal out her being home. I should have, and I would have normally, except all I could think of at that moment was how much I didn't want the two of them there. I could hardly wait for them to leave.

"What's up!" Tara said, pretending to be amazed. "It's our annual last-night-of-freedom partying time. How could you forget? Doug Mason's having a pool party, and we came to drag you away from this place."

"Yeah," Amy said, proudly holding a tote bag that looked familiar. "We even stopped by your house and picked up your stuff, so we can go straight to Doug's." She stepped up closer to me and whispered, "I can't believe you're still working here. I thought for sure you'd have quit before now."

I shrugged and smiled weakly as she sneezed and added, "Jenny, how can you stand it? It smells." She sneezed again. "I must be allergic to something in here."

"So you get off in five minutes, right, Jen?" Tara said, waving her car keys. "I'll go pull the car up front, and we'll meet you outside, all right?"

"Sure," I said, feeling like I'd just been blown over by a hurricane.

As soon as they left I turned to Mandy and begged her to watch my register while I ran back to the stockroom to tell Danny not to wait for me.

"Why should you care?" she said. "It's your last night anyway. What are they going to do,

fire you for leaving your register?" Mandy and
Laurie—and Danny too, of course—were all
staying on to work after school and weekends. I
was the only one quitting that night.

I ran through the aisles back to the stockroom, feeling like a prisoner set free. When I got
there, I looked around frantically, but Danny
wasn't there.

"If you're lookin' for Dan, he's helpin' unload
a truck out back," one of the guys said. "It's
gonna take 'im a little while longer to finish."

"Oh," I said, feeling confused and then relieved that I didn't have to face him. "If I write
him a note, will you give it to him?" I said.

The guy shrugged. "Sure."

I took a pen and crumpled-up register receipt
out of my smock pocket and scribbled a note:

> *Danny— Some friends showed up at the store
> to take me out. We always celebrate our last
> night of freedom before school starts.*

I stopped to think what to write next. I was
going to add *See you tomorrow*, but that's when
it hit me that the summer was over. Danny's
and my summer. I glanced at my watch and
knew I had to hurry before Amy and Tara came
back into the store to look for me. *See you
tomorrow at school*, I finally added, but I had a
funny feeling in my stomach as I did. *Love,
Jenny* I signed it, wondering what he'd make
of that, if he'd even notice. Then I punched out
at the time clock for the last time and practically ran out of Sav-Mor and into Tara's car.

Being with both my friends again was like
remembering something I'd forgotten or like
suddenly waking up from a dream. We talked

and laughed all the way over to Doug's. Actually, I mostly listened to Amy's and Tara's stories about their summers. Tara and I had talked a little bit over the summer, but it was different now that Amy was back. We always talked more and laughed more and just had more fun when all three of us were together. When there were only two of us, it was like a recipe with a missing ingredient.

Amy had met a lifeguard at camp who she really hoped was going to write to her. And Tara had already told me about two or three older guys at her mother's office who had flirted outrageously with her over the summer. Amy managed to pump more information out of her about them than I'd been able to. To tell the truth, I guess I hadn't tried very hard.

"What about you, Jen?" Amy asked as we pulled into Doug's driveway. "It must have been the pits working at that place, right?"

Tara smiled. "It's not exactly overflowing with guys you'd ever want to know, right?"

"No, not exactly," I said uneasily, realizing that I wasn't going to say anything about Danny *again*. That gave me a really creepy feeling. Keeping things from my parents was one thing. According to Danny, everybody did that. But what did it mean when I didn't even want my friends to know about a guy I really liked? It wasn't a good sign, I knew that.

7

THE NOISE in second-period geometry was reaching that "dull roar" that some teachers tell you to keep it down to.

"Jeremy, that is the grossest joke I've ever heard," Sara Samuelson shrieked. Then she laughed her famous laugh that shattered my eardrums even though I was sitting three rows away. I looked over and saw her flirting with the two boys on either side of her and trying to get the attention of a third. Typical, I thought.

Brad Loring crumpled up a sheet of notebook paper and tossed it into the wastebasket halfway across the room. "All right!" he and his basketball buddies yelled.

A stranger would never have guessed that half the biggest brains of the junior class (including Brad and Sara) were in that room, but it was true. We were all trying to enjoy our last few minutes of freedom before Ms. Rafferty showed up and the tardy bell rang. It was the second day of school. All the excitement of the first day was over, and it was time to face up to the awful truth: we were in for a whole new year of homework, tests, and making the grades.

But this year I wasn't thinking much about making the grades. All I could think about was Danny. I hadn't seen him at all the day before.

Well, that's not exactly true. I had seen him, and I think he saw me too, but he was with his friends walking down the hall, and I was with mine, and neither of us had said a word to each other.

I was hoping he'd wait for me after school, and maybe he did, but Amy and I ended up staying after awhile to talk to Mr. Remsen about the orchestra. Amy and I both play in the first clarinet section. Anyway, I looked for Danny's car as Amy and I left the building at four, but he wasn't there. Of course not, Jenny, I reminded myself. He has to be at work by four-thirty. I thought of stopping by Sav-Mor in case there was a chance of seeing him there. But I knew there wasn't much chance unless I went back into the stockroom. And I had too much pride to do that. Besides, I'd be embarrassed to be seen at Sav-Mor so soon after I'd quit. Like I couldn't stay away or something. I knew I couldn't face Mandy and Laurie either. I couldn't pretend like we were friends or anything. They wouldn't have fallen for that anyway. They would think I'd just come in there to show off because I didn't have to work there anymore and they did. Or worse, they'd suspect the truth, that I'd come in there to see Danny.

The sound of Jason Andrew's voice pulled me back in from the never-never land of my daydreams to the real life of geometry class.

"Hey, Jenny," he said cheerfully, "how was the Cape this year?"

Jason and I have been buddies for a long time. I had a terrible crush on him in the sixth grade when we worked on a science-fair project together, but I got over it. Now we're just friends.

"I didn't go this year," I answered. "My parents went, but I stayed home and worked. Last year I felt like the only person there over twelve and under thirty, so I skipped it this year."

"Where did you work?" Jason asked. "In New York with Tara? She said it was too much!" he adding, rolling his eyes. "With Tara around, I can believe it!"

"Um . . . no," I said, feeling embarrassed. "I just worked at Sav-Mor . . . as a cashier." I stared hard at him, daring him to make a nasty remark about Sav-Mor. I wonder if this is how Danny feels when he's challenging me, I thought.

Jason didn't laugh but he seemed a little embarrassed too. "Oh yeah?" he said, and then paused as if to give me a chance to explain why I had wasted my summer on something so worthless. I didn't.

"Oh . . . well," he continued, "I went to Technicamp. It's the best computer camp on the East Coast. I met a guy there who's got an idea for starting our own computer business. Lots of kids our age are doing it, so why not us, right?"

I smiled, wondering how I could ever have had a crush on Jason. He was nice, and cute too, but definitely not my type. Jason could have been a model for a preppy handbook. Blond and blue-eyed, he was wearing khaki pants, an oxford cloth shirt, and Topsiders. Boring, boring, boring!

Just then, Ms. Rafferty showed up, right before the tardy bell rang. She was kind of young, I guess, for a teacher, and kind of pretty, so lots of the boys liked her.

"Just what I like to see," she said, sighing and shaking her head, "a roomful of dedicated scholars in earnest pursuit of mathematical truth."

A wave of giggles swept through the room. I didn't think it was *that* funny. It was strange. Kids I'd known for ages were starting to irritate me lately. Either they seemed as old as their parents, like Jason, or else they seemed really infantile. I was the only person I even halfway understood anymore. And I wasn't doing so great at that either.

I didn't pay much attention in class that period, but I did hear Ms. Rafferty say something about how geometry taught you how to think better and solve problems more logically. I didn't have a clue what she was talking about. Flipping through my textbook, I wondered how isosceles triangles and obtuse angles—whatever they were—could have anything to do with anybody's real-life problems.

Everybody was pushing to get out of class at the end of the period, and when I got close to the door, I saw Danny leaning up against the lockers across the hall. Was he waiting for me? How did he know my schedule? He wasn't looking my way, so he hadn't seen me yet. I had almost decided to embarrass myself and call out his name, but before I could one of his buddies yelled his name from the other end of the hall.

"You, Ondich!" the guy boomed. I looked down the hall in the direction of the voice. A whole group of guys were walking toward Danny, the guys I'd seen him meet outside Sav-Mor once.

Danny yelled back, "Hey, Stefano," and joined his buddies. I was going in the same direction, so I was right behind them for a while.

"Got to watch out for those preppies, man,"

one of them said. "They'll walk all over you if you're not careful."

They all laughed, as if that was the funniest thing they'd ever heard. Danny laughed loudest of all.

"What's wrong with you?" Amy asked at lunch. "You're so quiet."

"Nothing," I said firmly. "It's just kind of strange, getting used to school this year. That's all. I'm excited for Tara, though, aren't you?" I added, changing the subject. Tara was going to be cheering in her first football game that week, and Amy and I had promised to sit in the pep section and cheer the loudest. I hoped talking about Tara would take my mind off Danny. I really did want to talk to somebody about him, but I knew Amy was the last person in the world I should tell. She'd never understand in a million years.

"Okay, I guess," Amy answered. "But I still don't get it. Why does she want to be one of *them*?"

I couldn't help laughing. "Amy, you make them sound like some kind of disgusting bugs or something. I mean, I don't want to be a cheerleader either, but who cares if somebody else does?"

Amy shrugged. "I don't know. It just makes me wonder, that's all. Want any of my potato chips?"

I sighed and said no thanks. Sometimes it seemed like Amy wanted everyone to be the same, like her. And that's not what I wanted at all. I mean, one of the reasons I liked Danny was because he was different from anyone else I knew. Because I didn't know what to expect from him. And that was kind of exciting. Amy would never understand that.

That afternoon Amy and I walked home together. She was coming to my house to try on some of my tops so she could borrow one for the football game on Saturday. She hated to admit it, but I could tell she was looking forward to the game. Even though Amy giggled a lot, she's really serious when it comes to school. Last year she used to make a big deal out of how much she hated the football team because they were just a bunch of dumb jocks who didn't deserve the attention of the whole school. But this year she seemed to be weakening.

"Eagles and Warriors," she was saying, as if they were the dumbest words she'd ever heard. "Who thinks up these things anyway?"

"What do you mean?" I asked.

"Eagles and Warriors. It doesn't make any sense. We're the West Branch Eagles and we're playing the Alliance Warriors. It's hard to think of eagles and warriors being enemies. Know what I mean?"

I sighed. "Amy, did anyone ever tell you that you take things too seriously sometimes?" I asked.

"Only you and my mother," Amy said with a smile. Then she sighed. "But who else would bother? Tara's so wrapped up in cheerleading she hasn't noticed us much lately."

That's when we both heard the car horn and looked across the street. It was Danny.

"What does *he* want?" Amy whispered. "We don't even know him."

I hesitated for a split second before I said, "I do. His name's Danny Ondich. I . . . met him this summer at Sav-Mor."

Danny was rolling down the window of his Camaro. "Want a ride?" he called.

"He's got to be kidding," Amy mumbled under her breath.

"Amy," I whispered, "I have to go. Do you want to come along?"

She shook her head slowly, staring at me in disbelief.

"Let's do the tops tomorrow, okay?" I said, wanting her to give me permission to desert her, wanting her to tell me it was all right. She didn't. "I'll call you tonight and explain everything, all right?" I said quickly as I checked for traffic and crossed the street.

"Hi," Danny said as I got into the car. "What's wrong with your friend?"

I looked out the window at Amy, who was still standing there frozen to the spot. I waved at her guiltily as Danny put his foot on the gas and took off.

"Oh nothing," I lied. "She just had a bad day and wants to be by herself." And in just a second I forgot all about Amy. I was back in Danny's car with the radio blasting and the wind whipping through my hair. We were back in our own little world, the world we'd made this summer, and I felt so happy!

"Want to get a burger?" Danny asked.

I thought about the chicken and rice my mother had asked me to start cooking by five o'clock. "Oh, well, sure, but, um, I sort of have to be home by five."

"Hey, that's okay," he said, grinning again. "I, um, sort of have to be at work by four-thirty, remember?"

"Oh, yeah, right," I said, laughing, as we

turned into the parking lot of the Burger King near the mall.

"Want to sit inside?" Danny asked.

"Sure," I said, wondering if anybody I knew from school would be there.

When we got inside, I told Danny I just wanted a Coke, and he stood in line while I went to find us an empty table. I kept thinking that five minutes before I had been on my way home to watch Amy try on tops and now here I was back with Danny again. Two different worlds. Two different *me's*. Strange.

The only table I could find was right next to a college-aged couple. That was too bad, because even though they were at a separate table, it was sort of attached to the one I sat down at. They looked so sure of themselves and so, I don't know, *together*. I wondered if Danny and I would ever look like that. The boy and girl glanced at me as I sat down, but I kept my eyes on Danny. I liked the way he stood in line with his hands in his pockets.

"Sure you don't want anything to eat?" he asked as he handed me my Coke a few minutes later.

"I'm sure," I said, smiling happily at him. It was like we hadn't seen each other in weeks, instead of just two days. He was glad to see me too. I could tell.

Then he just sat there eating his Whopper and staring at me for a few minutes. I sipped my Coke and looked around Burger King as if there was something interesting to see instead of the same old yellow and orange plastic furniture. Every time my eyes came back to Danny, he was still staring at me. I noticed the girl in the couple sitting next to us glance at Danny and then at me. What did she think? I wondered. Did we look like a "real" couple? We sure didn't sound like one, I knew that.

"How's school?" I finally said when I couldn't stand the silence any longer.

He shrugged. "Same as ever. I try to ignore it, you know?"

I nodded, meaning I knew what he meant, but of course I didn't. Not really.

"How's work?" I asked when I realized he wasn't going to say anything else about school or ask me how it was going for me.

He shrugged again. "Same," he mumbled, and then took another bite of his Whopper.

The same? How could it be the same without me? Didn't he miss me at all? I got really quiet. Why should I work so hard to talk to someone who didn't even miss me?

The couple beside us got up to leave. Sadly, I watched them walk away holding hands and laughing.

"Hey, what's wrong with you?" Danny said when he finally looked up from his Whopper long enough to realize I was upset.

I shrugged. "Nothing."

He pushed his knees up to mine under the table and stroked my hand gently with one finger. "So, want to meet me after work tonight?" he said, looking into my eyes and making me melt inside.

I sighed. "Danny, I can't go out at ten o'clock on a school night. There's no way my parents are going to let me. Besides, what would I tell them?"

He dug into his french fries without saying a word, but the message was loud and clear. What my parents thought and what I said to them was becoming a boring issue to him.

Finally he looked up again. "So, do you want to meet me or not?" he said, as if he hadn't heard anything I'd said.

"Danny," I said kind of desperately, "I can't. Don't you understand?"

He didn't say a word. He just got up and started leaving—without me! Just like that night in the Sav-Mor parking lot. I sat there in a daze for a second or two until it hit me that this time was different. This time I didn't have a ride home and it was miles from the mall to my house. So I jumped up and ran after Danny to the parking lot, feeling like a real jerk. I got to the car just as he was about to pull out.

I sat there catching my breath as Danny waited for the traffic to pass so he could get onto the highway.

"Are you going to take me home?" I asked timidly as he turned left.

"Hey, no, Jenny," he said sarcastically. "I'm gonna leave you here in the middle of the highway, all right?"

I kept quiet for a while after that. Then I tried again. "Why can't you understand? I mean, you know I can't see you after work much because I have homework and other stuff, and my folks say I need my sleep, but that doesn't mean we can't still see each other . . . at school and on weekends, right?"

"School, oh sure," he said, getting sarcastic again. "Look, Jenny, I like you, but I don't know if seeing you is worth fighting off all those preppy friends of yours you're always surrounded by, know what I mean?"

Sure I knew what he meant, and I wanted to

scream something back at him about his creepy friends too. But I didn't. And I realized something. I would gladly (well, maybe not gladly exactly) put up with Danny's friends if that's what I had to do to see him, but he would never put up with mine. That was just the way it was.

We were both quiet until he pulled up a few doors away from my house and let me out. Then he pulled one of his classic Danny changes, just like magic. "Hey," he whispered, almost smiling, almost nice again, "don't worry. We'll figure something out. I'll see you tomorrow, okay?"

"Okay," I said, leaning over the seat to kiss him on the cheek. "Bye," I said happily as he left. I really was happy again. Over such a little thing. After all that. Unbelievable.

Amy was very quiet when I called her that night.

"I'm really sorry about this afternoon, Amy," I said.

"It's okay," she said unconvincingly.

"I had to go, Amy. I had to. I . . . like him. A lot."

She didn't say anything.

"Amy?"

"What?"

"Don't you have anything to say?"

"What can I say, Jenny? He's *your* boyfriend, right? It's none of my business."

"Come on, Amy, don't be a pain. Give him a chance," I pleaded. What I wanted to say was something about how scared and alone and mixed up I felt, how much I needed a friend. But I couldn't admit how torn up inside I felt about Danny. I had to act sure about him, so Amy would have a good impression.

"I hope he deserves you, Jenny. That's all I can say."

"Want to come over tomorrow and try on the tops?" I said, changing the subject.

"Sure," she said with absolutely no enthusiasm whatsoever.

That word was starting to become a joke as far as I was concerned. Everybody said "sure" about a hundred times a day, but nobody really seemed sure about anything. Especially not me.

8

"GUESS WHO gave Jenny a ride home from school yesterday?" Amy announced at lunch the next day.

"Who? Who?" Tara squealed in excitement, staring at me.

"Danny somebody," Amy said. "What's his last name again Jenny?"

"Ondich," I mumbled, not looking Tara in the eye.

There was silence for a few seconds after that. Then Tara finally said, "Oh . . . I think he's real cute, Jenny . . . except I didn't think he was your type."

"Turns out they had a hot love affair at Sav-Mor this summer, can you believe it?" Amy said with a little laugh. "Jenny was holding out on us."

I remembered what Danny had said about "preppy types," and I was furious with Amy for proving him right. "You don't know one single thing about him, Amy," I sputtered, "so why don't you just shut up."

Amy cleared her throat. "Um, maybe I'll just leave now," she said quietly. "I have some homework to finish up by sixth period anyway. Bye, Tara." She picked up her tray and was gone.

I stared down at my tray and poked at my food.

"I can't believe it," Tara said, shaking her head. "I don't see you guys for a couple of days, and suddenly you've got a new boyfriend, and you and Amy are enemies."

"We're not enemies," I insisted. "Amy just doesn't understand."

Tara hesitated. Then she said softly, "Do you really like him, Jenny? I mean, like, *really* like him?"

I shrugged. "I don't know. I'm not really sure," I admitted. "But I at least want to give him a chance, Tara. Amy's problem is she won't give anyone a chance. She thinks she knows so much about everybody, only she doesn't. Not about Danny anyway."

"Doesn't he hang out with Mark Stefano and all those guys?" Tara asked. She was too nice to say what she thought of his friends, but I knew. And I agreed with her about them.

I sighed. "I don't know. I guess. But does that really matter? He doesn't act like them, Tara. Not at all. And maybe with me . . . oh, I don't know. At least he's not boring, like some boys I could name."

"Jim Peters isn't boring, I can tell you that for sure," Tara said, her eyes twinkling.

"Who's he?" I asked

"The senior guy who wants me to go out with him after the game this week," Tara announced, beaming.

"Tara, that's terrific! What's he like?"

"Well," Tara began, taking a deep breath, "he's gorgeous for one thing, and he's already been accepted early decision into Princeton, and he's *so* nice."

We talked about Jim until the bell rang. And it was sort of like the old days. Only Amy should have been there. And maybe I shouldn't have been comparing Danny to Jim so much, wondering why Tara and I had picked two boys who were so different.

That afternoon Danny asked me to the football game. Sort of. He didn't ask if he could take me. He asked if I wanted to meet him there. I was walking out of geometry when I saw him waiting for me. I knew it was an important sign. He wasn't going to avoid me in school anymore.

"Hi," I said softly, happily, when I saw him.

"Hi," he said, acting real casual. "So, listen, are you going to that football game tomorrow?"

"Sure," I said, looking down the hallway for any signs of his friends—or mine. "You probably have to work, right?"

"No, old Wiseman is actually giving me the night off, so I thought I might check out the game. I don't think we have much of a chance against Alliance but you never know."

We were actually walking down the hall together in plain view for the whole school to see! I don't know which of us had decided the direction to go in, but luckily it was the right one for me.

"Well, I go to all the games. My friend Amy and I are going to sit together in the pep section this year. Our friend Tara's on the cheerleading squad," I explained.

"Hey," he said, taking my hand, "why don't you sit with me this week instead? My car's messed up, but I could get a ride and meet you there. What do you say?"

"What happened to your car?" I asked. "It was okay yesterday."

"Ah, nothing really," he said. "Some old lady hit me in the Sav-Mor parking lot and knocked the front end out of line. So, tell your friend you're gonna be with me tomorrow night, right?" he said insistently, coming back to the subject of the game.

He was still holding my hand, and I just stood there like a jerk in the middle of the hall, not saying anything, wondering if I could change my plans with Amy. And then, suddenly, Danny was kissing me, really kissing me, on the mouth, right there in the hallway! People were passing by us and lots of them seemed to be staring at us. I knew because I had my eyes wide open. Two girls from my English class went by and called, "Hi, Jenny." I just blushed.

"Hey, come on, say yes," Danny insisted, squeezing my hand, after I'd finally pulled away from him.

"Okay, yes," I said nervously, and then he suddenly let go of my hand.

"Good," he said softly, in the voice that always made me melt. "See you tomorrow. Meet you at the front gate where they take the tickets, okay?" Then he dashed off down the hall.

Amy and I already had plans to go to the game together. Her father always went to every home game, so he was giving us a ride. I could never get the family car the night of the games, because my parents usually had plans, and besides, they knew Amy's father could take us. If Tara hadn't made cheerleader that year, we all could have gone together in her car—unless we had dates of course. We all understood that getting a date with a boy could sometimes change our plans. If it had been any other boy but Danny, I knew Amy would have understood.

Any other boy would have been willing to sit in the pep section with me and Amy, too, I reminded myself. Well, maybe not *any* other boy, but lots of boys would. The kind of boys I was used to dating would.

Amy had a doctor's appointment that afternoon, so we didn't walk home together. I helped my mom get dinner that night, and then my parents and I watched "Dallas" together on TV. By the time it was over, it was ten o'clock, still early enough to call Amy and tell her about Danny. But I was tired. And I just didn't want to.

"I think I'll go to bed," I said to my parents. "I'm exhausted."

"Rough week, honey?" my mother asked sympathetically.

"Kind of," I dodged. "Good night, you two."

"Good night," they both called, looking up from their reading. Dad was reading a magazine about camping gear. Mom was studying the want ads. She was always looking for secondhand bargains, garage sales, and flea markets. They both looked so calm and relaxed, like they had no idea what it was like to lie to the people you love. Of course I wasn't really lying. But there was lots of stuff I wasn't telling them.

I didn't sleep well that night. I had all kinds of strange dreams. And the next morning I felt kind of groggy as I was having my toasted waffles. When the phone rang, I almost jumped out of my chair.

"Hello," I mumbled sleepily.

"Hi!" Amy said cheerfully. "All psyched for tonight?"

"Oh, sure," I said guiltily. *Tell her*, a voice inside me urged.

"We'll pick you up at seven, okay?" Amy was saying.

"Okay," I agreed. "See you then."

That Saturday was not one of my best days. I helped my dad clean out the garage, and then Mom made my favorite Saturday lunch—home-made pizza. My parents seemed real happy that day. Sometimes they act real young, like they're in love or something, and usually I like it. But that day I couldn't stand it. Why wasn't I that happy? I wondered. I was in love, wasn't I? Then why did I feel like I was about to take a big test I had forgotten to study for?

Amy was positively bubbling when I got into her father's car that night. I'd never seen her so excited about a football game before.

"Jason Andrews says we don't have a chance tonight against the Warriors, but I think he's wrong," Amy said with a grin. "I bet him five dollars we'd win."

Her father and I both looked at her in disbelief. Then her father smiled at me over Amy's head.

"*You* made a bet on a football game?" I said.

"Sure," Amy said, full of spirit. "Jason thought he was so smart. I couldn't let him put down the Eagles. With us cheering for them, they can do anything, right?"

Suddenly that's just what I really wanted to do—sit next to Amy and cheer my lungs out for the team. At that moment Danny seemed totally unreal. I wasn't sure whether he was really going to be at the front gate waiting for me or not.

Amy's father parked the car and turned to us. "I'll meet you ladies here after the game.

Don't be late, understand?" He tried to sound kind of tough, but we both knew he was a cream puff deep down. Besides, sometimes we ended up getting a ride home with friends anyway. If that happened, all we had to do was find Amy's father and let him know.

"Okay, Dad, we'll be here. No problem," Amy said.

Then her father left, and Amy and I fixed our hair, using the car windows as our mirror.

"Amy, there's something I have to tell you," I began nervously.

She looked up at me, and her smile turned to a frown.

"What's wrong?" I said.

That's when Danny came up from behind me and stood between us. "Hi," he said to me. "I was standing by the gate and I saw you get out of the car." Then he turned to Amy. "Hi," he said.

"Hello," Amy said coldly. Then she stared hard at me, waiting for an explanation.

"I'm going to sit with Danny tonight," I said, trying to sound cheerful, but feeling like a jerk. "You don't mind, do you?" What could she say?

I turned to Danny. "Want to sit in the pep section with Amy?" I said hopefully.

"Pep section?" Danny said, as if he didn't know what one was. "Hey, see, my buddies are saving us great seats in the top row of the bleachers. They're waiting." He looked at Amy, then at me. "Come on, Jen," he said. "Let's go."

I looked at Amy guiltily as Danny took my hand and pulled me away. "I'll meet you at the concession stand at halftime, okay?" I said.

She didn't say a word. She just kept looking at me.

* * *

I forgot all about Amy as Danny and I walked
along to find his friends. It felt great to have
him holding my hand and talking to me, while
all the pre-game noise and excitement went on
all around us. We walked by Tara as she was in
the middle of a cheer, but she didn't see us.
Still, seeing her added to the good feelings that
were finally starting to grow inside me.

"Hey, you look good," Danny said, squeezing
my hand tighter.

"Thanks," I said, suddenly feeling very shy.
"Still think Alliance is going to win tonight?"

"Hey, really," he said, "we don't have a chance.
Jeff Simms, the only good quarterback we got,
is out with an injury. So you can forget our
passing game right there."

"Oh," I said, feeling disappointed. He made it
sound like the game was over before it even
started. I watched him scanning the tops of the
bleachers, looking for his friends.

"We could always sit by ourselves somewhere,
I guess," I said hopefully.

"Don't worry," Danny said, "we'll find them."

Just then I heard loud voices that sounded
like people cheering for the team. But it was
Danny's friends, trying to get his attention. Five
of them had stood up in the top row of the
bleachers and yelled his name. People all around
them were turning and staring. I looked up to
where Danny's buddies were and saw that some
of them had girls sitting with them too. I recognized a few of the girls from my gym classes,
but I didn't really know any of them.

Danny yelled something back to his friends
and said, "Let's go" to me. Still holding my
hand, he led me up to where his friends were

sitting. It wasn't easy getting to the top of the
bleachers. We had to step around a lot of people
or ask them to move, and I ended up smiling
apologetically to a lot of them after Danny had
pushed his way through, but finally we got there.

"Hey, everybody, this is Jenny," Danny said.
They all looked up, but they didn't really pay
much attention to me. Danny and I sat on the
end of the top row. He was on the very end. I
was next to Mark Stefano. On the other side of
Mark was his girlfriend, Tina.

I noticed that way down below on the field
the game had started, but nobody in the group
seemed to be paying much attention. The boys
would glance up from time to time when somebody was running with the ball. The girls mostly
talked among themselves.

Danny was leaning forward around me to talk
to Mark about his car. It sounded like they had
spent all day working on it.

"You two need a little warm-up?" Tina said,
turning to me with a smile and handing me a
paper bag.

I took the bag and looked inside. There was a
quart bottle of wine in there. We were all underage, and, besides, drinking wasn't allowed at the
games. Anyway, the only drinking I'd ever done
was having a few glasses of champagne at my
cousin's wedding the summer before.

"No thanks," I said, handing it back to her.

"Hey, wait a minute," Danny said, grabbing
my hand. "Don't worry, I'll take care of our
share." He took a drink and passed the bottle
back to Tina. Then he put his arm around me.
"Having fun?" he said, looking at me very closely.

"Sure," I said, uncertainly.

"Hey," he said, "come here a minute," and he
pulled me closer.

"What?" I said, confused.

"This," he said, kissing me on the lips right there in front of all his friends and anybody else who happened to be looking our way. Kissing in public seemed to be a big thing with Danny now that school had started, and I had to admit it was kind of exciting, even if it was awfully embarrassing. It was so different from the summer; though. Everything in the summer had been so private, so secret. And I'd kind of liked it that way. I was so mixed up!

In the middle of the kiss, I heard everyone scream "all right!" and I looked up to see what was happening. People were getting to their feet all around us. The Eagles had just scored a touchdown.

"See?" I said softly to Danny. "I bet you we're going to win after all."

But I was wrong. That was the Eagles' first and last touchdown of the game. Not that anyone in "our" group paid much attention. They were too busy passing another bottle of wine and talking. Dan talked mostly to Mark. He didn't kiss me again, but he held on to my hand for most of the first quarter. Mark tried to talk to me a few times, but I didn't encourage him.

At the end of the first quarter, the other girls got up to go fix their hair and their makeup. Tina asked if I wanted to go along, but I said no. I wondered what they would say about me after they left. Anyway, once they were gone that left me alone with Danny and three boys I didn't really know—and didn't want to know.

"Let's get out of here at the half," Mark said as soon as the girls were gone. "We won't miss anything, that's for sure. I know a great spot we can show the girls."

One of the other guys laughed. "Or they can show us, you mean," he said.

I pulled my hand away from Danny's, suddenly nervous. Was he going to leave the game too? Did he expect me to go with him? Neither of us said a word about it until the second quarter was almost over.

Finally, when there was only a minute left on the scoreboard clock, Danny turned to me and said, "Want to go for a ride? We could get you back in time to meet your friend after the game."

I didn't say anything. I'd heard the expression "gut reaction" before, but I never really knew what it meant. Now I did. It was the feeling telling me I didn't want to go with them. But I didn't want to say no to Danny either.

"Let's go for a walk," Danny said, taking my hand. "Hey," he called to Mark as we started down the bleachers, "I'll meet you at the car in five minutes, okay?"

"Sure, later," Mark said, but by that time he was paying more attention to Tina than to us.

"What's wrong?" Danny said when we were alone. It sounds funny to say we were alone when we were surrounded by a couple thousand noisy football fans, but that's how it felt. I was staring at the ground as we walked along, wondering who had to clean up all the greasy pizza plates and crushed styrofoam cups.

"I don't know," I said.

"Don't you want to go?"

I took a deep breath and told the truth. "No," I said. "I don't."

Danny looked disappointed. But for once he didn't push it. "Okay," he said. "No problem."

I started cheering up, thinking how much

fun we'd have watching the rest of the game after all his friends were gone. Then I realized we were walking toward the parking lot. "Aren't you staying?" I said, suddenly knowing that he wasn't.

"I can't," Danny said. "I got a ride here with Mark. If they all leave, I won't have a ride home. This is his car here," he said as we came to a beat-up old Mustang in the dark parking lot. "I better wait for him."

I tried to imagine Amy's father taking Danny home and knew it would be a mistake. "You mean you're going with them . . . and their girlfriends . . . by yourself?"

He shook his head and grinned at me. "Hey, get serious, Jenny. That wouldn't be too cool, would it? Nah. I'll just have Mark drop me off at my house. Meanwhile, though, I gotta show you what you're missing, right?"

We were leaning against the side of the car, and suddenly Danny was kissing me again. If only it could always be just like this, I thought dreamily.

"Hey, I'll see you on Monday, okay?" he whispered, playing with my hair a little bit.

"Okay," I said. "I better get back to the game and find Amy." I suddenly remembered that I'd promised to meet her at the concession stand at halftime, and halftime was probably almost over by now.

I ran to the concession stand and looked for her, but she wasn't there. Then I ran toward the pep section and searched the bleachers for her face. It wasn't hard to find her. She was the one person in the stands who wasn't laughing and having a good time. Suddenly I was really angry at her. Why was she acting like such a baby? When was she ever going to grow up? Okay, maybe I should have told her about Danny sooner, but what was the big deal?

"Hi," I said, determined to be nice, as I squeezed in next to her in the bleachers.

She just looked at me.

"I'm sorry I missed you at the concession stand," I said. "Want some of my Coke?"

"No thanks," she said. "I had one while I was waiting for you." She looked away for a few seconds, as if she were watching something down on the field. Then she finally burst out, "Jenny, where were you? I was worried. What was I supposed to tell my father if I couldn't find you at the end of the game?"

That did it. "Amy," I said, "what is your problem? You knew I'd be there at the end of the game."

She gave me a hard look. "No," she said. "I didn't know that, Jenny. I don't know anything about you anymore."

That made me so angry I was afraid to speak. We were both quiet for a minute as the game started up again. I knew Amy must be wondering why I was staying in the pep section, but she didn't say anything for a while.

Finally, she turned to me. "Well, aren't you going back to sit with your *boyfriend*, Jenny?"

"I can't," I said quietly. "He left."

Amy looked shocked. "You mean he took off and left you here when you were supposed to have a date?"

"Well," I said, wanting to defend Danny, but not knowing exactly how, "it wasn't really a date, and he had to go because he needed a ride with his friends, and he did ask if I wanted to go along . . . but I said no."

"Gee, they really have a lot of school spirit, don't they, Jenny?" she said sarcastically.

I wanted to yell back at her something like, "Yeah, well what's so important about rah-rah school spirit and cheering for the football team anyway?" The trouble was, though, that I agreed with Amy, not with Danny. It bothered me a lot that he and his friends could just walk out in the middle of the game like that. But I couldn't admit that to Amy. So I didn't say anything.

The Eagles lost that night, just as everybody but Amy and me seemed to expect. We hardly said a word as we walked to the parking lot. But we had to wait a few minutes for Amy's father once we got to the car. Amy was so quiet, and I kept wondering what she was thinking. Finally, she let me know.

"I don't know, Jenny," she said, and I could tell she was trying hard not to cry. "I was really looking forward to this year, you know? But it's not turning out the way I expected at all. What's happening to us? We used to be so close, and now I feel like I don't know you at all anymore."

I folded my arms across my chest and stared at the ground, not saying a word.

9

MONDAY WAS the pits. Amy was barely speaking to me. And sometimes she gave me this look that made me feel like Frankenstein or something. I was so mad at her for overdoing it and not even trying to see my side of it that I couldn't even try to make up with her. Tara was busy hanging out with the other cheerleaders. She didn't seem to have much time for us lately. Amy was right about that. And I didn't see Danny the whole day. That was the worst. I hate to admit this, but I wouldn't have minded Amy being mad at me so much if Danny had been around.

I was feeling pretty sorry for myself by the time orchestra practice rolled around last period. I felt like nobody really understood me—or cared. Plus I had tons of homework to do that night, and to top it all off, Amy and I had signed up to take the SATs together in a few weeks. Mrs. Rubins, the guidance counselor, had called us into her office that afternoon and suggested we start preparing ourselves for the test. She handed each of us a huge book all about it. The closest Amy and I had come to being friends again had come when we looked at each other behind Mrs. Rubins's back as we carried those SAT books away.

All through orchestra practice I'd been thinking back to the summer—those lazy days with nothing to do but run a few errands and think about Danny, or better yet, take off to someplace special with him. Even Sav-Mor didn't seem so bad now that I thought about it. At least it had been easy.

Luckily, the clarinets didn't have much to do that day. Mr. Remsen spent almost the whole period going over and over a tricky piece that the trumpet section couldn't get right. So I could let my mind sort of drift in and out of class.

Toward the end of the period, I had just finished playing a piece with my section, laid my instrument down in my lap, and started to let my mind wander again when I saw Danny lounging in the hallway outside the open door to the orchestra room. He was grinning at me. And I grinned back. And just like that all my problems seemed to float away. Because I knew that in a few minutes I'd be in Danny's car again and everything would be all right, for a while anyway. I didn't even mind when I noticed Amy staring at us and frowning. Danny and I had something special that Amy just didn't understand. I couldn't help that. It was her problem, not mine.

"Hi," Danny said, talking real fast and almost running down the hall as I came out of class. With my clarinet and my homework and the SAT book, it was hard to keep up with him. He wasn't carrying anything, of course.

"Listen," he said, picking up more speed, "I got to hurry 'cause I'm getting a ride with Mark. See, my car's still messed up, so I need a ride to work with him, but he can't pick me up cause he's gonna be over at Jack's tonight. So can you pick me up at ten?"

It was the same old Danny challenge that I knew so well. It was like a test that had only one right answer: yes. It didn't matter if I had homework or what my parents thought about it. He wanted me to choose him. And I *wanted* to choose him.

"Okay," I sighed. "I'll pick you up at Sav-Mor at ten."

"Hey, great," he called, running out the door, "we can go over to Jack's and check out his new VCR."

"But I can't," I said weakly, long after Danny was gone.

I didn't say a word at dinner, but my parents were talking a lot about their jobs so they didn't really notice. I excused myself before dessert, saying I had a lot of homework to do, and they didn't seem to mind that either. Sometimes they like being alone anyway, I can tell.

I didn't even look at the SAT book that night, but I did get all my English done and most of my geometry, even though I kept looking at the clock every five minutes. By nine-thirty I have to go downstairs and tell them . . . something, I thought. What if they don't let me go?

At nine-fifteen I changed clothes, combed my hair, and put on a little more blusher. Then I grabbed a sweater and went downstairs, feeling like I was about to face a firing squad.

My parents were sitting at the kitchen table going over the family budget with a calculator and a legal pad open to a sheet full of numbers. On no. What bad luck, I thought.

My mom looked up from the calculator when

I walked in. At first her mouth and eyes had that tense, grouchy look she gets whenever she and dad talk about money. But that changed to surprise when she saw I was dressed to go out.

"Where are you going at this hour, Jen?" she asked.

"Um . . ." I hesitated and then pulled out a chair and sat down. "I have to pick up a friend from work," I said, not looking at either of them. "Okay if I take the car?"

"What friend?" Mom snapped before Dad had a chance to say a word. I could tell she knew already. Somehow she knew.

I took a deep breath and let it out. "Um, it's Danny, the guy at Sav-Mor, the one I went out with this summer, you know." I still wasn't looking at them. "His car's messed up, so he needs a ride home from work. He asked me at school today if I could pick him up and I said okay."

There was deadly silence after that, and when I finally looked up, my parents were sending each other some kind of signals across the table, deciding my fate.

"What's going on, Jen?" Mom finally demanded. "I thought you stopped seeing this Danny weeks ago."

I shrugged and tried to think of something to say. "Not exactly," was all I could come up with. She got really quiet after that and that's how I knew how angry she was. My mom doesn't scream and yell at you when she's mad; she gets real quiet instead. But you can almost feel her holding herself back.

That's when Dad broke in. I heard him fishing the car keys out of this pocket, and I couldn't believe it. They were going to let me go!

"Okay," he said to Mom, "Jenny's made a commitment which I think we have to let her keep. There's no point in leaving the boy stranded." He tossed the keys to me. "Don't be late, Jen. This *is* a school night," he said sternly. "And we'll discuss the other issues involved here tomorrow. Understood?"

"Okay," I said humbly, rushing out of the room. "I won't be late, I promise. Bye."

Dad answered me, but Mom didn't say a word. She didn't give the silent treatment very often, but when she did, it was deadly.

I felt like a robot as I started the car and pulled out of the driveway, like somebody else was pushing all the buttons and controlling me. I wished I was back in my room under the covers, reading about the SATs.

I parked in the darkest, most faraway corner of the Sav-Mor lot, the way Danny always used to, and waited for him. When he walked out of the store with Mandy a few minutes later, I watched them cross the parking lot. Danny was telling her a funny story—something he never did with me—and they were both laughing. I felt like they were both strangers, like I was watching a movie starring two unknown actors, people who had nothing to do with me. Then Danny opened the car door and got in.

"Hi," he said casually.

"Hello," I said in a little voice, playing for sympathy, I admit.

"What's wrong with you?" he asked, but he sounded more irritated than concerned.

"Nothing," I lied, wanting him to figure out that "nothing" really meant *everything*, wanting him to see how upset I was, wanting him to ask more questions, to care.

"Good, drop me off at Jack's, okay?"

I had the key in the ignition and the motor running but when he said that I got so angry I knew I couldn't drive, so I turned off the motor and sat there staring straight ahead.

"Now what?" Danny said in disgust. "What is your problem anyway?"

"You are!" I screamed, turning in the car seat to look at him. "You're my problem! I practically had to beg my parents to let me do this, and you don't even care. You're not even glad to see me. You just want me to drive you somewhere because no one else would do it, that's all."

"Hey, thanks a lot, Jenny. You really know how to make a guy feel great, you know that? So if I'm such a big problem for you, then why do you hang around? Huh?"

We both stared straight ahead into the parking lot, which was deserted by now. Neither of us said a word, and it was very, very quiet. Last summer we'd had some of our best times just sitting in this empty parking lot, but now everything was totally changed. The Danny and Jenny who had gotten together in the summer were like two people in a dream.

Danny reached out and put his hand on mine. "Hey, come on," he said softly, "can't you ever just lighten up a little? Come on over to Jack's with me. We don't have to stay long. I'll just have a beer with my friends, and we can watch part of a movie or something, okay?"

"Okay," I said unhappily.

There were two other cars in the driveway when we got to Jack's house. Jack's parents were hardly ever home, Danny explained, so that was where they all liked to hang out. The house was almost totally dark, but we could hear sounds from inside as we rang the front bell. We had to try two or three times before Mark finally answered the door.

"Hey, Dan, you made it, man," he said with enthusiasm. "Hurry up, you're missing the best part." Then he looked over Danny's shoulder and saw me. "Oh, hi," he said. I just smiled, sort of. I wondered if Mark remembered my name or even remembered meeting me at all.

He was leading us into the living room, and Danny was pulling me along by the hand. The only light in the room came from the TV set, but when I looked around I could see a boy and girl lying together on the couch, another couple making out on the floor, and three boys sitting in a corner drinking beer and grinning, their eyes glued to the TV.

I looked at the screen and saw two women with hardly any clothes on kissing the same man and taking his shirt off, and I knew right away what kind of movie it was. I gave Danny a panicked look that said "take me out of here," but he was too busy talking to Mark—and watching the movie—to notice.

Mark had just handed Danny a beer, and Danny was pulling me toward an empty couch when I broke free and said in a loud voice, "I'm going home." And I turned around and left. For once, I didn't care what any of them thought or whether Danny followed me or not. He didn't.

My mother was in bed when I got home, but Dad was waiting up for me in the living room.

"Can we talk a minute, Jen?" he said as I called good night and started up the stairs to my room.

Oh please, Dad, not tonight, I begged him with my eyes. But he didn't pay any attention.

"Come on in and sit down a minute," he said, using his "reasonable" voice, but also pulling on the ends of his mustache the way he always does when he gets nervous. My dad has curly blond hair and always has a good tan because he plays tennis and hikes a lot. My friends say he looks really young and handsome, considering he's over forty, but he's just my father to me.

I sat down in a chair across from him and stared at my feet.

"So," he teased gently, "how does it feel to be sixteen these days?"

I frowned and looked up at him. "Not so hot, okay? Can I please go to bed, Dad? I'm awfully tired. Maybe we can do this tomorrow, like you said before?"

"No, wait a minute, just wait a minute, Jenny," he said firmly. "This won't take long. I just want to give you something to think about in the meantime. About your mother."

"What about Mom?" I asked, rolling my eyes and not really wanting to hear.

"Well, you know, your mother was a lot like you when she was your age, at least when I met her in college, that is."

"What do you mean?" I asked, slightly curious.

"Well," Dad said with a smile, "she tended to go for the guys who were a little bit on the wild side, a little unconventional."

"Like you, for instance?" I teased.

"As a matter of fact, yes," Dad returned. "You've seen the pictures of me, Jen. I was quite the hippie in my day. And your mother's parents were not crazy about the idea of her taking up with me, let me tell you. She had to put up quite a fight."

"Grandma and Granddad didn't like you?" I asked in amazement.

"Let's just say it took them awhile to get to know me," he said with a smile. "And then you came along, and I settled into my serious, responsible mode and everything eventually fell into place. Anyway, the point I want to make is about your mother. You see, she knows what it's like to be in your place, and she's trying real hard not to make the mistakes her mother made with her. She wants to understand, Jen, she really does. And she's willing to be tolerant—within limits of course. We both are. But you've got to give us a chance. If your mother makes the effort to put herself in your place and tries not to come down too hard on you, but you feel like you have to go sneaking around anyway, how do you think that makes her feel?"

I honestly didn't know what to say. How could I tell my father that how my mother felt was the least of my worries that night? How could I tell him that maybe they wouldn't have to be "tolerant" much longer anyway, because after what happened that night I wasn't sure I even wanted to see Danny again. They'd never believe that now, I realized. Not after I'd already lied about it once.

I sighed and said the only thing I could think of that might satisfy my father. "I'll think about it, Dad, okay? Can I go to bed now?"

"Good night, Jen," he said, looking tired himself. "Sleep well."

"You too," I called on my way upstairs.

What a joke. I hardly slept at all that night.

*   *   *

The next morning I lay in bed listening to my parents bustling around getting ready for work. I was trying to wait until they'd gone before I got out of bed so I wouldn't have to talk to them.

"Jen," my mother called as they were leaving for the train station, "it's seven-thirty. You'd better snap to or you'll be late for school."

"I'm up, Mom, thanks," I called down the stairs.

"Okay, honey, have a good day," she called back, as if nothing had happened the night before.

"You too," I returned, trying to sound the same way, but not quite succeeding.

When I ventured down to the kitchen, there was one of my mother's notes on the fridge:

> Jen,
> Your father and I would love to meet Danny. Why don't you ask him to dinner at our house? How about Friday night?
>
> > Love,
> > Mom

Oh fabulous, I thought. How am I ever going to get out of this one?

10

I WAS writing a geometry proof on the board the next day when Danny appeared outside the door and called my name so that I could hear, but Ms. Rafferty, who was talking to someone in the back of the room, couldn't.

"Hey, Jenny," he said in a loud whisper, "come here."

I shook my head, mouthed the words "I can't," and then looked back in Ms. Rafferty's direction.

Danny looked there too, then shrugged and crooked his finger in the way that means "come here." I was about to tell him to meet me after class when Ms. Rafferty noticed him and came marching to the front of the classroom. I turned back to the geometry problem, hoping to stay out of what was going to happen. Ms. Rafferty liked me. It wasn't fair of Danny to get me in trouble with her.

"Can I help you, young man?" she said, sounding a little tougher than usual.

"I doubt it, " Danny said to my amazement. Everyone in the class heard him and there were a few stifled giggles.

You could tell Ms. Rafferty was embarrassed and angry and maybe a little nervous. It gave me a funny feeling to imagine a teacher feeling scared of Danny.

She walked out into the hall and asked Danny if he had a pass. When he said no, she walked back into the room, told those of us who had put problems on the board to explain them, and said she'd be right back. Then she marched Danny off to the office.

My cheeks were burning hot as I explained the geometry proof to the class. Nobody in geometry knew about Danny and me, but that didn't really matter. It was bad enough that I knew.

Amy tried to be friends again at lunch, but I had so much on my mind I couldn't put much effort into being friends back.

"Hey, Jenny," she said, "why don't you come over to my house after school on Friday and we can hang out for a while and then see a movie or something?" Her eyes looked as hopeful as her voice sounded.

"I can't, Amy," I said sadly, thinking of the dinner my mother had planned for Friday. "I'd like to, but I can't. Maybe next week, okay?"

I knew she figured that the reason I said no had something to do with Danny, and it did, only not the way she thought. If only I could explain it all to her, I thought. If only I could make her understand.

"Sure, Jenny," she said in that sarcastic way that was starting to really get to me. Then she picked up her tray and left.

I felt so alone after that, and when Danny slipped into the chair next to me a few minutes later, I didn't feel much better.

"Hi," he said, casually as usual, as if nothing had happened.

"Hi," I said, surprised that he wasn't

still angry about what had happened that morning—or the night before.

"You didn't tell me this Rafferty fox was such a flake," he said, grinning.

"She's all right," I insisted, "and she's not exactly a fox—or a flake."

"Hey, look, she's not much older than we are, right? I'm not going to let her push me around."

I looked away from him for a moment, knowing there was no way we could ever agree about Ms. Rafferty, hoping Danny would at least not show up to bother me during that class again.

"So what was so important?" I finally asked. "What was so urgent that you couldn't wait till after class to tell me?"

"Hey, look," he answered, "I just wanted to say I was sorry about last night, okay? I should have known you wouldn't like it there. Just like you don't like anything my friends and I do."

I started to say that wasn't true, but it was. And besides, what kind of apology was Danny really giving me? It sounded more like he was blaming me.

"So what happened in the office?" I asked.

"Ah, they gave me detention, Friday after school. I'll have to miss work or get there late. Maybe I'll just call in sick. I could use a night off anyway."

"Oh," I blurted out, suddenly remembering my parents' invitation.

"Oh what?" Danny asked.

I sighed. "My parents want you to come to dinner on Friday. They want to meet the boy who's ruining their daughter. But I guess you can't come, huh?" I said hopefully.

"I don't know. Is your mother a good cook?" Danny asked, teasing me.

"My mom and dad are both good cooks," I said proudly, hoping that would surprise him.

But he ignored that fascinating bit of information.

"Sure, why not? As long as it's after five," he said. "Can you pick me up here?"

I was amazed that Danny was actually accepting the invitation. I'd thought I'd have to talk him into doing it—for my parents' sake. This sounds crazy but I think he wanted to do it because he could see how nervous the whole idea was making me. It was another one of his challenges.

"My parents don't even get home till six-thirty, remember? And I guess I can pick you up."

"Gee, you really sound thrilled about this," he said. "What's the matter, don't you want me to come? I thought you wanted everything to be all nice with your parents."

"I did," I said, feeling confused. "I mean, I do," I corrected myself.

In movies and books lots of times there's a scene where a girl brings her boyfriend home to meet her parents, and usually it's supposed to be funny. I mean, you know everybody is nervous and everything, but that's kind of what makes it funny—at least to the person reading the book or watching the movie. I guess you're supposed to think that the girl will think it's funny too, when she looks back on it later in her life. But the feeling I had in the pit of my stomach Friday afternoon wasn't funny at all, and even if I live to be a hundred, it won't seem any funnier. I'm positive about that.

Mom had decided we should have something

"fun" for dinner to "break the ice." First, she suggested tacos, but I vetoed that right away. The thought of us all sitting around a table with sour cream and taco sauce dripping down our chins was like a nightmare. Then she suggested shish kebab, cooked on the barbecue grill outside and that sounded better. It was almost October, but it was still warm enough to eat outside. And I actually liked putting the shish kebab together, which was my job to do before Mom got home.

All I had to do was cut up some meat and some slices of onion and vegetables and then slide them onto long skewers. It was the kind of job you could do and still think about other things, the kind of job I usually like. That day, though, the only other thing to think about was Danny. Why did my parents have to invite him over this week when everything was such a mess between me and him? Things are always a mess between you and Danny, a little voice inside me said. But I ignored it as I put the shish kebab in the fridge and picked up the car keys and went to pick up Danny from detention. I'd told my parents that I had to pick him up, but I hadn't said from where.

The house was quiet when Danny and I walked in, but I could tell my parents were home and had been working in the kitchen.

"They must be out back," I whispered nervously to Danny. "Come on, I'll introduce you."

"Hey," he said, grabbing my arm as I started to go, "why don't we just wait in here for them?"

He was reminding me of those times, those secret times, when we'd been alone in the house together, and I felt helpless to get him to act the way I thought he was supposed to act when he met my parents. All I could do was give him a look that said, "Danny, please, please, don't mess this up."

That's when my mother rushed in from out back at exactly the wrong moment and saw the expression on my face. In a split second she looked worried but she covered it up quickly and was her typical polite "company" self just as if I always brought home unsmiling boys with purple streaks in their hair.

"Hello," she said cheerfully, waiting for me to introduce Danny.

"Mom, this is Danny Ondich; Danny, my mom," I said quickly, getting it over with.

Danny just sort of nodded his head at her instead of saying something polite back the way he was supposed to. But my mom got a big smile on her face—too big—and said, "It's good to meet you Dan. Hope you like shish kebab." She kept looking at him cheerfully, waiting for him to make a polite reply that would keep things going.

Danny just shrugged. I could tell he wasn't used to being polite to other people's parents. He didn't know the automatic answers you were supposed to give to a question like that. "Sure, I guess," he finally said. "I never had one, not that I know of."

"Well," my mom continued, gathering plates and utensils and stacking them on a tray, "it's one of Jenny's favorites."

She looked brightly at me, as if it was my turn now to say something pleasant and polite, but she must have seen that I wasn't up to it, because she dropped it right away.

"Why don't you take Dan out and introduce

him to your father, Jen? And then the two of you can just relax until dinner." She opened the refrigerator and said, "Can I offer you a cold drink, Dan?

I gave him a panicked look that said, "Please don't ask for beer, *please*." I knew my parents wouldn't like that.

"Coke? Sprite? Seven-Up?" my mother continued, saving the day by limiting the choices.

"Um, sure," Danny said without any enthusiasm. "Coke is okay, I guess."

My father was brushing sauce on the shish kebab and turning them on the grill as they browned.

"Daddy, this is Danny," I said, turning around to make sure Danny was still there.

Dad set down the basting brush and took off the potholder mitt he was wearing on his right hand. "Glad to meet you, Dan," he said, shaking Danny's hand and staring mainly at Danny's punk haircut—trying to figure out if he could be a criminal, I guess.

Shaking hands seemed to be another thing Danny wasn't very used to. He seemed really embarrassed afterward and looked at me for a clue about what to do next. The look on his face made me feel very protective and almost sorry for him. I was amazed again at how changeable Danny could be. I remembered how tough and sure of himself he'd acted at the bar in New York. And now he was falling apart in front of my parents. My parents! Unreal.

"Let's go over to the table," I said, taking him by the hand even though I felt very shy about touching him in front of my parents. I hadn't felt that shy with other boys in front of my parents, but then touching Danny was different than touching other boys I'd known. Everything about him was different.

The first thing Danny did when we sat down was to light up a cigarette. That would be another strike against him in my parents' eyes, I knew. They both used to smoke but they'd given it up once they decided that being healthy was so important. Now they didn't even like people to smoke in our house and always hid the ashtrays to discourage them.

That didn't stop Danny. He just grabbed a styrofoam cup and started flicking ashes into that. I prayed that it wouldn't catch on fire.

We didn't have much to say to each other even when my parents weren't around. I mean, the whole situation was so artificial, so different from what we were used to when we were together.

"The shish kebab is usually good," I said, sounding as cheerful and phony as my mother had a few minutes ago. "I think you'll like it."

He raised his eyebrows and grinned, as if to say, "Who cares? This is so unreal."

Danny and I were sitting together on one side of the table, and my parents sat down on the other side once they'd brought the food over. That meant I had to spend most of my time looking at them and seeing the expressions on their faces—the bright, cheerful, phony expressions. I knew I was being unfair to them, that they really were trying for my sake to make this work, but knowing that didn't make it any easier to get through the dinner.

My dad tried to talk to Danny about music. "Jenny says you're really into rock," he said enthusiastically. "I notice a lot of old-timers, like Tina Turner and Mick Jagger, are really

making a comeback these days. What do you
think of that?"

Danny didn't say anything for a few seconds,
which is a long time in a conversation. Then he
looked up from his plate, shrugged, and said,
"They're okay, I guess." Before my dad could
ask him another question, Danny took a big
bite of food that took a lot of chewing and
looked away from the table, staring down at the
grass as if there was something fascinating
there. It seemed like making conversation with
adults over dinner was another thing Danny
had missed out on. I didn't know who to feel
sorrier for—my father, who was trying so hard,
or Danny, who didn't seem to know how to.

My mother and I talked for a while after that,
about what was going on at school and stuff
like that. Then Mom turned to Danny, who had
already finished everything on his plate, and
offered him more food. "I'm afraid we only have
two kebabs left, Dan, but you're welcome to
them," she said politely. "I'm not used to feed-
ing a teenage boy, you know. Jenny hardly eats
anything these days."

Once Danny finished the last of the shish
kebab and was looking around nervously with
nothing left to eat, my mother started asking
him about his family, how many brothers and
sisters he had and stuff like that.

When she started asking about what his parents did, I tensed up. I didn't know the answer,
but I knew it was going to be something a lot
less classy than being a lawyer or an editor,
and I knew Mom was going to pretend not to
notice that, and that all of us would know that
she was just putting on a phony act. Suddenly I
remembered Danny saying, "Yeah, well, your

mother is full of shit," and I wished real hard
that Mom wouldn't ask him what he wanted to
do after high school.

Danny said his parents worked at a canning
plant out by the highway, and my dad started
asking him all these complicated questions
about whether production was down and whether the union was renegotiating its contract,
and of course Danny didn't know anything about
that stuff. He said all he knew was that as far
back as he could remember his parents had
both been laid off for most of the winter every
year when the plant slowed down and that he'd
rather clean toilets than take a job there himself.

It was an awful moment, and in the deadly
silence that followed, we all stared down at the
table and the only sound was the scraping of
forks on our plates. It's very hard for me to
admit this, but mixed in with all my feelings
about how horribly things were going and how
bad my parents must feel was a little flash of
triumph that somebody had finally said something that totally shut my parents up. I guess it
was almost like I had done it myself.

My parents cleared the plates a few minutes
later and brought out dessert, which we all ate
in silence. When they cleared those dishes away
and went inside, Danny turned to me and said,
"So, can we get out of here now?"

"Okay, sure," I said, relieved that it was all
over. "Let's go."

My parents pretended to be disappointed when
I announced I was taking Danny home.

"Oh," my mother said, "it's too bad you have
to go. I hope we see more of you after this."

It sounded pretty phony, but in a way it was
true. It didn't necessarily mean she liked Danny

and wanted me to keep on dating him. It just
meant that if we were going to keep seeing each
other, then she expected him to come to our
house and pick me up.

"Good to meet you, Dan," my father said,
shaking hands again. "Next time I expect you
to fill me in a little more on the music scene.
I'm serious about that."

"Sure," Danny said with a shrug, and then
looked expectantly at me, telling me with his
eyes to get him out of there. Luckily for him, I
was better at reading his moods than he was at
reading mine.

In the car, Danny didn't say anything—good
or bad—about meeting my parents. When we
got to his house, he didn't invite me in. He
didn't even want me to pull into the driveway.
It was like *he* was ashamed of *me* or something. I blushed in embarrassment and anger.

"See you," Danny said casually as ever as he
got out of the car and slammed the door.

"Bye," I said softly, then I went home.

11

ON SUNDAY my parents dragged me along on a hike with them. That's something we used to do together a lot when I was younger. The two of them still went hiking a lot, but I hardly ever went with them anymore. I can usually think of better things to do on Saturday mornings. Sleep, for instance.

They'd suggested the idea the night before, after I'd come back from driving Danny home. They tried to make it sound like it was no big deal, but I knew what was going on. Mom wanted to "talk"—about Danny. She thinks people can say things to each other out in the woods that they can't say in real life. When I was eleven, that's where she told me about the facts of life and announced that I was about "to become a woman." Well, it worked when I was eleven, but it wasn't going to work that day, I vowed. I didn't want to "talk" anymore. I just wanted to be left alone.

But I said I'd go anyway. It seemed easier just to say yes instead of "discussing" it and explaining my reasons for not going. Just because I went along didn't mean it had to turn out the way they wanted.

Still, lying in bed the next morning, I considered backing out. A few minutes later, though,

Dad was knocking on my door, calling me to breakfast. "Get 'em while they're hot, Jenny! I'm just about to pour the pancake batter on the griddle."

"Okay, Dad, in a minute," I grumbled sleepily. He sounded so excited that I felt guilty. He'd be disappointed if I said I didn't want to go. I wonder if I'm a freak or if all "only" kids are so afraid of letting their parents down.

When I walked into the kitchen, Mom was packing the trail lunches while Dad made breakfast. "Good morning, Jen," she said cheerfully. "The trail should be spectacular today. The leaves are really at their peak."

"Uh-huh," I said, going to the refrigerator for the orange juice. I couldn't figure out why they were so excited about leaves. We had a whole front yard full of leaves that I'd probably have to rake. Of course, being in the woods is different than being in your front yard, but still, I didn't know what all the fuss was about. Maybe it's because they spend all week working in New York City, I thought. That would be enough to make anyone ready for the woods, I supposed.

"Hope Danny enjoyed the dinner," Mom said as she passed me the syrup.

"Oh . . . sure," I said uncertainly. Then I smiled, for her sake. "It was nice, Mom. Really."

Then I stuffed my mouth full of pancakes so I'd have an excuse not to say anything for a while.

Mom took the hint and started talking to Dad instead. "So, what do you have planned for us today, oh fearless leader?" she asked.

Dad rubbed his hands in excitement. "I thought we'd head for Almost Perpendicular

Mountain. I know that's one of Jenny's favorite spots and we haven't been there in years. The view should be terrific today. Think you're up for the climb, Jenny?"

"Sure, Dad," I sighed, and saw my parents exchange looks.

"I'm going upstairs to get ready," I said as soon as I finished my pancake.

Mom looked me over. "Aren't you ready now?" she asked.

I gave her a look. "Mom," I sighed, "look at me. Look at my hair. Look at my face. I can't go out like this."

She laughed. "Jennie, we're just going to the woods. Nobody's going to be looking at you there. Besides, there's no point in wearing makeup when you're just going to get all sweaty anyway."

I sighed. "Mom, do you mind? I'll only be a minute. You guys aren't ready yet anyway."

Dad was deep into the sports section of the Sunday *Times* by then and wasn't paying any attention to us.

My mother is hopeless when it comes to stuff like makeup. It's not like she thinks I'm too young for it or anything like that. It's just that she doesn't like to wear much of it herself, so she doesn't understand why I do. *I'm not like you!* I keep wanting to tell her, but so far I haven't come right out and said that.

Dad was right. Almost Perpendicular is one of my favorite spots. It gets its name because one side of the mountain goes almost straight up and is just about impossible to climb. We usually go up the other side, though, which is just hard enough climbing to be fun. At least, that's how I felt about it when I was ten or eleven.

Luckily, my parents didn't bother me much in the car. They were listening to the radio and discussing some restaurant they used to go to when they were young and lived in New York. So that meant I could lean against the window in the backseat and think my own thoughts as the scenery whizzed by.

I closed my eyes and thought about kissing Danny. He was the most exciting boy I'd ever known, that was for sure. But Amy didn't like him. So what? Did all my boyfriends have to be approved by Amy? Deep down, I wondered if she was just jealous.

My parents didn't like Danny either. I knew that. Even if they pretended to accept him, I knew they really wished I'd find somebody else, somebody different. They probably thought if they acted "reasonable," then I'd get over Danny. But I didn't want to get over him. I thought about all the bad things that had happened with Danny. And all the good things. The times he'd made me mad or hurt my feelings. And the times he'd made me feel so warm and good. The times he acted so tough. And the times like last night when I wanted to protect him and make everything all right. The more confusing things got with Danny, the more I wanted to make them right. If only he could change, just a little. . . .

"How are you doing back there, Jenny?" Dad asked after a while, catching my eye in the rearview mirror.

"Great, Dad," I answered automatically.

"Well, here we are," he said, pulling into the parking area.

"You guys go on ahead," I said to my parents as we started along the trail. "I feel kind of lazy today. Don't worry, I can follow the trail markers."

"Sure, honey," Mom said, looking disappointed. "Just yell if you need any help."

Give me a break, please, Mom, I thought, gritting my teeth. Why would I possibly need help?

She and Dad set off down the trail together, holding hands. They really did seem happy lately, I thought. That was good, I guess. Good for them.

I sat down on a rock and watched a shower of yellow leaves float to the ground. It was real quiet for a minute, and I felt kind of peaceful just sitting there. I waited till my parents were out of sight. Then I started walking, kicking the brightly colored leaves that had piled up along the trail, the way I used to when I was ten.

When I got to the base of the mountain, my parents were waiting for me.

"Ready for the perilous ascent?" Dad joked.

I smiled and thought about it. I knew the climb would be fun, but something in me resisted. I know it sounds mean, but at that moment I just didn't want to make my parents happy. I knew they really wanted me to climb with them, and that's why I said no.

"I don't know, Dad. I'm still feeling kind of tired. I think I'll take this easy trail that winds around the mountain instead. I'll meet you guys at the top, okay?"

I don't know. Maybe I was testing them a little, even then, seeing how much they'd let me break away from the way they wanted me to be. It was a small thing, a dumb thing really, but I did it anyway.

"Are you sure you'll be all right, Jen?" my mother asked.

"I'll be all right, Mom," I said with my teeth clenched. Then I added, "I think I'll just walk along and enjoy the scenery, okay?" I knew she'd like that answer. As long as I was enjoying the leaves, everything was still okay, she'd figure.

Mom smiled. "Okay, honey, see you at the top. Make sure you work up an appetite, though. We've got bagels and cream cheese and a thermos of soup for lunch."

On the long trail up the mountain, I started feeling guilty—and a little lonely. Why couldn't I just enjoy myself? My parents weren't really that bad. And they were trying, I knew that. What was wrong with me?

When I reached the top of the mountain, they had already spread out a red-checkered tablecloth on the rocks and were pulling the food out of their packs.

"Welcome, stranger," my father called when he saw me coming. "Pull up a rock and have a seat. The view is even better than I remembered."

I sat down and looked around. He was right about that. It felt nice to be up so high, to look down at all the yellows and reds and oranges of the trees below. I could see other mountains in the distance, and the clouds looked so close I felt like I could reach up and touch them. A hawk sailed by, riding the wind with its long outstretched wings. I remembered how when I was ten I always wished I could become a hawk so I could know how it felt to fly like that. Watching the one in front of me then, I felt that way again.

Just then I heard some music and turned my head. On another part of the mountain, I could see a bunch of kids, girls and guys, about my age.

"Oh, no," my mother sighed. "Why do those kids have to spoil such a beautiful, peaceful place with their radios?"

"It's a free country, Mom," I said without thinking.

"Well, I like music too, but this isn't really the place for it," she said, handing me a thermos cup of soup.

"They're just having fun, Mom," I protested, my voice getting louder, "and they're not hurting anyone."

"Looks like they could very well hurt themselves, though," Dad commented. "I see they've got a few six-packs of beer with them. Seems to me it's pretty dangerous to be sitting on a cliff getting drunk."

They were both right in a way. It did kind of ruin the mood to have that loud music playing. And it was pretty stupid to drink beer on a cliff. But weren't those kids allowed to have fun too? Did everyone who climbed a mountain have to be exactly like us?

"Well, I guess it's really not any of our business," I said, putting on my windbreaker. It was getting cold up there.

Neither of my parents said anything more about it. We all took the easy trail down together, but everyone was pretty quiet.

On the way home, Dad asked me if I wanted to stop at the local farmers' market.

"Halloween's coming up soon, and we haven't gotten a pumpkin yet. Want to help me pick one out, Jen?"

"Sure, Dad," I said without much enthusiasm. That was another thing I used to love when I was ten, I thought a little sadly.

I acted a lot younger than ten at the farmers'

market. I knew how infantile I was being, dragging behind Mom and Dad, refusing to smile or give any other answer than "I don't care" to their questions, but I couldn't seem to stop.

When we got back into the car and had driven for a few minutes, Mom suddenly turned around in her seat, and I couldn't help sighing in dread of what was coming.

"I wish you'd tell us what's on your mind, Jen," she said, looking concerned. "Maybe we could do something about it. I know you think we overreacted back there on the mountain, but parents just do that sometimes. We remember all the foolish things we've done and how lucky we were to survive some of them, and we can't help feeling protective. Maybe a little overprotective, huh?" She was smiling a little, asking *me* to understand *her*.

I closed my eyes and sighed again.

"Hey, Jen, come on," she said softly.

"Mom," I said through clenched teeth, "I'm sixteen, and there's nothing you can do about it. Nothing. You're not sixteen, and you're not me, and you don't know what it's like, so stop saying you do."

I heard her turn around, and when I opened my eyes, Dad was staring at me in the rearview mirror, but he didn't say a word.

12

"I DON'T know what to do, you guys. Everything always starts out great with Danny and me, but then it gets messed up somehow." I didn't want to talk to my parents about Danny, but I was finally ready to confide in my friends. A little.

I picked up a wooden spoon and stirred the chocolate chips I was melting in a pan on the stove.

"He really took you on a mystery date in New York?" Tara said. "It sounds kind of exciting." She opened the jar of marshmallow cream and handed it to me.

I looked over at Amy before I said anything else about the date. She was chopping walnuts at the kitchen table and didn't seem to be paying any attention to us.

"Well," I sighed, "it was kind of exciting, for a while anyway. But then we got thrown out, which was my fault, really, for looking like such an infant."

I dumped a blob of marshmallow into the chocolate, stirred it around, and dipped my finger in to taste the result.

It turned out Amy was listening after all. "Sure, Jenny," she said in disgust, looking over at me. "Blame yourself as usual."

"Here," Tara said, taking the pan of fudge over to Amy. "Dump those nuts in and have a taste. Maybe it'll sweeten up your personality."

Amy tasted the fudge, reluctantly. "Well, somebody has to tell Jenny the truth," she said.

"And what is the truth, oh master?" I said, walking over to her and bowing.

Tara giggled.

But Amy didn't even crack a smile. "The truth is you're wasting your time with this guy, that's what. He's just not worth it."

That stopped all the kidding fast because the real truth was that once in a while the exact same thought had sneaked into my mind but I'd always gotten rid of it. Now Amy had said it out loud.

"Hey, Amy, why don't you give Jenny a break, huh?" Tara complained. "It's real easy for you to say what she should do, because none of this is happening to you. But lots of times figuring out how you feel about a guy just isn't that easy. And sometimes there's stuff about him that nobody knows but you, and you wouldn't even tell your closest friends, right Jenny?"

"Yeah," I said, a little surprised that I wasn't the only one who felt that way. Did Tara really have secrets about her boyfriend too? "Wait till you have a boyfriend of your own, Amy," I continued. "Then you'll see."

I really believed what I was saying, but I wouldn't have said it if I hadn't been pretty mad at Amy for making me feel bad about Danny. I guess I wanted her to feel bad too. Or at least for a minute I stopped caring whether I hurt her feelings or not.

"Thanks a lot, Jenny," Amy said. "From now

on I'll know that my opinion doesn't count—
unless I have a boyfriend."

Tara sighed. "Hey, come on, you guys," she
said. "How did boys get into this anyway? This
is *our* night. It's tradition. We can't spoil it
with all this dumb stuff about boys. Let's light
the jack-o'-lanterns, okay?"

We put on our jackets and headed out to my
front porch with the three pumpkins we'd carved
after school. Tara was right. Spending Halloween night together was a tradition with the
three of us. We'd done it ever since the fourth
grade.

We set up the jack-o'-lanterns on the sidewalk facing the house and lit them. Then I
turned out the porch light, and we sat huddled
together on the top step of the porch and
watched the candles flicker in the crazy faces
we'd carved. Later on, we would put the pumpkins up on the porch railing, as usual, and
they'd light Amy and Tara's way down the sidewalk as they went home. Then I'd blow out the
candles, as usual, and go to bed.

"You know," I said, "I still think my parents
are crazy for liking this old house better than
new ones like you guys live in. But I sure would
miss this old porch if we ever moved."

"Me too," Tara said.

"Remember how it used to be on Halloween?"
Amy said softly in the darkness. "We'd just be
going out about now and our bags would get so
full of candy that sometimes they'd break?"

We all laughed at the memory of Amy's bag
breaking on a dark sidewalk and the three of
us scrambling to find all the candy and stuff it
into our pockets so she could get it home. We'd
stopped trick-or-treating after the fifth grade,

but I remembered those days so well. Tara would always dress up as something that allowed her to wear pretty clothes and makeup, like a princess or a ballerina. Amy would usually go as a hobo or a witch. I was the one who always tried to think of something different. Once I went as a banana and another time as a can of Raid.

"It's not like that anymore," Amy said sadly.

"That's because we're not kids anymore," Tara said.

"No, I mean it's not like that for kids anymore," Amy answered. "Now their parents are afraid to let them go out at night by themselves, so they all go trick-or-treating right after school. And they only go to houses where they know the people because they're afraid people will stick things in the candy. It's terrible."

"Yeah, we were pretty lucky, I guess," I said. "We sure had fun back then."

We were all quiet for a while after that. Then Amy said, "I'm sorry I said that about Danny, Jenny. I just don't like it when you put yourself down every time you talk about him."

"Okay," I sighed. "I'm sorry too. But Tara's right. There's a lot you don't know about him. I wish you could see him the way I do. He's not like those other guys he hangs out with. Not at all. And he's so free, you know? He doesn't care what other people think. He just does what he wants. I kind of like that."

"Well, I admit I wish I could be like that sometimes," Amy said. "Maybe you can have him talk to Ms. Stein for me."

"What do you mean?"

"It's so gross I can't even stand to talk about it," Amy said. "Remember when we had to write those stupid essays about 'Democracy' at the beginning of the year?"

"Yours wasn't stupid," Tara said. "It was good. Remember you let me read it to get some ideas for mine? Only you got an *A* and I got a *C*, so I must have missed something."

I laughed.

"Well, anyway," Amy continued, "Ms. Stein liked my essay too. She liked it so much she wants me to read it at the Thanksgiving assembly."

Poor Amy! I thought, grateful for once that I wrote lousy essays. "Can't you get out of it?" I asked. "She can't make you do it, can she?"

"Well," Amy said, "she can't threaten to expel me or shoot me or anything like that, but you know Ms. Stein. She can make it awfully hard for you to say no. She's already told me how much she's counting on me and how I have a 'real contribution' to make to the school and garbage like that."

"Hey, don't worry," Tara said. "It's not that bad being in an assembly. You get used to it. I'm finally getting used to being in the pep rallies and cheering at the games."

"But I'm not you, Tara," Amy complained. "And reading an essay on Democracy isn't like doing cartwheels at a pep rally either."

That's when we heard the motorcycle pull into the driveway. We all looked up at the headlight coming toward us in the darkness.

I had a feeling it was Danny, but I wasn't really sure until he walked over to the porch and took off the helmet he was wearing. Till then, it was kind of spooky to have someone in a helmet and dark clothes pull up to my house on Halloween night.

"Hi," he said when he was standing in front of us. He seemed kind of shy in front of my friends. The three of us were sitting close together on the top step, and Danny didn't seem to know whether to stand or sit or what.

"Hi," I said. I pointed to a lower step. "Have a seat."

"Hi, I'm Tara," Tara spoke up. "Is that your cycle?"

"Uh, I borrowed it from a friend, and I have to bring it back," he answered. "I just came by to see if Jenny wanted to go for a little ride. Do you?" he said, turning to me and trying to make eye contact in the dark.

"Well . . ." I started, and then hesitated. I felt like a big magnet was pulling me away from my friends and toward Danny. But what about our Halloween tradition? What about all the stuff we'd been talking about? I hadn't felt so close to Amy and Tara in a long time. Why did Danny have to come along right then? You can say no, Jenny, I reminded myself.

"Go ahead, Jenny, don't mind us," Amy said, and I wondered whether she really meant it. I couldn't tell.

"If you don't go, I will." Tara giggled.

"Okay," I said, jumping up. "But I'll be right back. You guys wait here, okay? And if my parents get home . . . tell them I'll be right back, but don't mention the motorcycle unless you have to."

Once I decided to go, the only thing I felt was scared. I'd never been on a motorcycle before. Danny handed me the helmet. "Here," he said, "you take this. There's only one." I liked feeling his hands around my face as he helped me put it on.

Then he got on the bike. "Watch out for this pipe," he said, pointing down. "It's real hot and can burn you bad if you let your leg touch it. "Now all you have to do is squeeze in behind me and hang on tight."

When he started the engine and I felt all that power underneath us, I was suddenly terrified. It was like that moment when the roller coaster starts up and you realize it's too late to change your mind and ride the ferris wheel instead.

Danny kept to the back roads, so there wasn't much traffic. After a while, as we rode up and down the lonely country roads, it almost felt like we were the only two people in the world. It was nice.

Then he turned off into the woods on a dirt path. Luckily, there was a full moon that night to light our way. He pulled up to a lake and turned off the engine.

"Hi," he said. "Cold?"

"A little," I said.

"Like the ride?"

"I loved it."

"Come on," he said, getting off the bike. "Let's take a walk."

Suddenly I realized we were out in the middle of nowhere in the dark, and I felt kind of nervous. Danny led me by the hand to a big rock that overlooked the lake. As we climbed to the top I wondered for a second whether he'd brought other girls here before. Probably he had, I realized. We sat quietly on the edge of the rock and watched the path the moonlight made on the lake.

"This is my favorite spot," Danny said.

"It's nice," I answered. The rock was icy cold against my jeans, but I didn't want to complain.

He put his arm around me and kissed me softly. "How come I'm always telling you I'm sorry?" he whispered into my hair. He looked at me and ran his finger under my chin.

I didn't know what to say.

He stared out over the lake. "You know the best thing about New York?" he said softly. "Nobody's watching you. Nobody knows you and nobody cares what you do. It's great."

I cleared my throat and finally spoke up. "I know what you mean. I felt kind of like that when we were there."

"You did? I thought you hated it."

"I didn't hate it. I was just worried about being in that place and getting home, that's all."

"Hey, Jenny, you got to stop worrying so much about stuff. I mean it," he said, looking out at the lake. "It's not worth it. Just do it, that's what I say."

That was the big difference between Danny and me. I worried about everything: what my friends thought, what my parents thought, what Danny thought, whether I could get an *A* in geometry, whether I'd get into a good college. Part of me liked Danny because he didn't worry about anything like that, but I could never really be like him, I knew that.

"I bet you're even worried right now, aren't you?" Danny said, putting his hand on my leg.

I felt myself tense up as soon as he touched me and I knew he could feel it too. I shrugged. "Kind of," I said.

"What are you so worried abut, Jenny?" he asked. It was one of his challenges again.

I sighed. "I don't know. I'm worried about what my friends are going to say when we get back. And whether my parents are home yet. And . . ." I couldn't admit the real thing I was worried about.

"And what I'm going to do right now?" Dan asked, putting his arm around my waist.

I looked away from him. "Not really," I said. "Maybe I'm more worried about myself, because I'm not sure what I want to happen."

"You know, I really hate it the way you're always so worried all the time," he said. "It makes me so mad sometimes. Like why should you care? Why should either of us care what anybody thinks?"

There were tears in my eyes, but I hoped he couldn't see them. "I know," I said. "You're probably right. I wish I could be the way you want me to be sometimes. But I'm not. Can we go now?"

He didn't move or say anything for a while. He just stared out at the lake. "No you don't," he finally said, in a mean voice.

"No I don't what?"

"Ever wish you were more like me. Just the opposite. You hate the way I am, really. But you keep thinking I'm gonna change or something. And be more like you, Little Miss Perfect. Only I'm not."

"I don't think I'm perfect," I said softly. "Far from it."

Danny turned to face me. "You think you're better, though. Better than me anyway."

That stung, because I couldn't really deny it. It was true in a way.

"I thought you liked me," I whispered, hating myself for sounding so pathetic. "I thought maybe we were even in love."

"Love," Danny said in contempt. "It's just a

joke, didn't you know that? It's just something girls read about in books. It doesn't have anything to do with real life. Everybody knows that. How dumb can you be?"

At that moment I felt pretty dumb, all right. I felt like the dumbest person who ever lived. Like I didn't know anything anymore. Not a single thing.

"Can we go now . . . please?" I begged. "I'm freezing."

When we got back, my friends were gone, but my parents weren't home yet. I'd lucked out again.

Tara and Amy had left the jack-o'-lanterns lit and the candles had burned almost all the way down. I blew them out and went upstairs.

As I took my shower I wondered whether I was going crazy. Sometimes lately I felt like there were three different Jennies—three different me's. The person I was with Danny, the person I was with my friends, and the person I was with my parents. Then I suddenly remembered a Jenny I'd forgotten: the one I was right now in the shower all by myself. The most important Jenny of all. What was happening to her?

13

ALL THE next week, Danny and I seemed to be playing a game. I tried to avoid him in school because he'd really hurt my feelings, and I wanted him to come to me and apologize. To show he really cared. But it turned out he was avoiding me too. And when I passed him in the halls, he'd give me a look that was half mean and half sad, as if I was the one who'd done something wrong, as if he was the one whose feelings had been hurt.

And since he worked nights, there wasn't much chance of him calling me, but still I waited every night by the phone, trying to concentrate on Shakespeare or chemistry problems.

On Thursday that week, my parents stayed in New York to see a play. I could tell Mom was a little worried about me when she called from her office at five o'clock.

"Hi, Jen," she said in her overly cheerful voice, the one that was a dead giveaway that something was wrong. I wondered if Mom's legal opponents could read her as easily as I could. I guess not, or she wouldn't have a job. She went through her usual questions about how school was that day, reminded me how much nutritious food there was in the fridge, and then asked me if I had any plans for the evening.

"Yeah, Mom," I said sarcastically, "I was planning to go out and rob a bank tonight." We both laughed a little nervously, and I realized that the old jokes about me doing something outrageous weren't as funny as they used to be. I mean, obviously I wouldn't rob a bank or anything like that, but Mom and I both knew I was capable of lying to her, of having secrets.

"Maybe you should invite Amy over to keep you company," Mom suggested tentatively. But she knew Amy and I weren't as close as we used to be. Halloween night had been an exception.

"I'll think about it," I said. We both knew that was a lie. Finally I said, "Hey, Mom, I'm fine, okay? I'm going to do my homework, watch a movie on TV, and go to bed, all right? Don't worry so much."

"Okay, we'll be home around midnight, all right?" Mom said brightly.

She was still worried, I could tell, but probably Dad had convinced her it was the right thing to do. I could just hear him saying something like, "We can't watch over her like a jailer, Susan. And we can't totally give up our private life, either." It was true, and I don't blame them for not being home that night. But I still can't help wondering what would have happened if they'd been there.

I had finished my homework and was settling down in front of the TV when Danny called. He was drunk. I could tell that right away.

"Hi," he said in a sexy voice when I picked up the phone. "Can Jenny come out and play?"

"Where *are* you?" I asked, feeling like his mother. "What's going on?"

"We're gonna have some fun. I'll be right over," he said, and hung up.

I quickly flung off my bathrobe and pajamas and slipped on a blouse and a pair of jeans. Then I sat in the living room watching the minutes tick by on the clock on the mantelpiece. At nine-thirty I heard the squeal of brakes in the driveway and then Danny leaning on the front doorbell. When I opened the door he was there with Mark and Mark's girlfriend Tina.

"Jenny, they're crazy. You have to do something," Tina pleaded. "I'm not riding with them." She was drunk too, but not as bad as Danny and Mark. Danny was hanging all over me and laughing a lot even though there wasn't anything funny. Mark was looking around my house as if he didn't have a clue where he was.

"Here's the keys. Come on," Danny said, pulling me to the door. "We're gonna have fun. But Tina wants you to drive."

"Can't you drive?" I asked Tina, not wanting to go along, but knowing it wouldn't be safe to let Danny or Mark behind the wheel.

"It's a stick shift," Tina complained. "I never learned that. Come on, Jenny. You have to help. He's your boyfriend."

She was right. I had to. I'd never driven a Camaro before, but our family car was a stick shift. That's what I'd learned on. For a few seconds I tried to figure out if there was anything else I could possibly do. But I knew I could never get Danny to just stay put for a while. If I didn't decide to drive right then, they'd just leave without me.

Once I was settled in the driver's seat with Danny in the seat next to me and Tina and

Mark in back, I turned around to ask Tina if she knew the way to Danny's house.

"I've only been there once," I explained, "and Danny was giving me directions the whole time. I know it's a turn off Leonia Boulevard, but I can't remember which one."

Before she could answer, Danny said, "I'm not going home. We're gonna have some fun."

"Danny, I'm taking you home, then I've got to get back before my parents get home." But if I dropped Danny's car off at his house, how would I get home? Maybe Tina could drive me in her car somehow?

'I'm not leaving this car until we have some fun," Danny insisted, and I believed him. Sometimes in the movies they make drunk people seem funny, but this wasn't funny at all. Danny could be hard to deal with sometimes, but I'd never seen him like this before. In a way it was like he wasn't there at all, like someone else had taken his place. It scared me.

"I want to go to the mall," Danny said. "I want to have some fun at the mall."

"Okay," I said, humoring him. Glancing into the rearview mirror, I could see that Mark was already asleep on Tina's shoulder. Maybe if I just drove around awhile, Danny would snap out of it, I thought.

The mall was just about ready to close when we got there, but Danny insisted we all go inside anyway.

"But Mark is asleep," I reasoned with him. "Even if we can wake him up, he's gonna be pretty groggy."

"Okay, you and me then," he said, grabbing my hand and pulling. "Come on. Let's have some fun."

I followed behind him as he lurched into the mall through Sears, feeling like I was caught in a nightmare I couldn't control.

"Look, Danny," I said, running to catch up with him in the aisle, "they're getting ready to close up. We might as well go home, right?" I tried to sound gentle and reasonable, the way you do when you're trying to coax a five-year-old into doing something.

Danny looked around in confusion until he spotted a can of spray paint in the automotive department. "Hey," he shouted, his whole face lighting up, "I want to paint my car. It needs a touch-up. I have to buy some red. Got any money?"

I shook my head no in disgust and then waited off to the side while be bought the can of spray paint. Maybe he'd leave now, I thought. Maybe he'd let me take him home.

Danny seemed strangely excited by the time we got back to the car. "Hey, Stefano, wake up," he yelled to Mark in the backseat. "We're gonna have some fun now." But Mark was still dead to the world.

"Drive to the school," Danny ordered me.

Then I put it together. The spray paint. School. "Forget it, Danny," I said. "I'm not getting mixed up in this."

Tina wasn't saying anything. She wasn't helping me one bit.

"Then get out and let me drive," Danny said. "You're no fun, Jenny. That's your problem."

I winced at that and wondered whether Danny was doing all this just to get back at me for being "Little Miss Perfect."

I started driving to the school very slowly to

give myself time to think. If I'd gotten out of the car, I'd have been stranded at the mall, and what if Danny got in an accident? Maybe if I stayed, I could still stop this somehow. I tried to catch Tina's eye in the rearview mirror, but she seemed to be asleep now too. Unless she was just pretending.

As soon as I pulled into the school parking lot, Danny jumped out of the car with the spray paint. "Hey, Stefano, you coming?" he called to Mark, who was snoring in the backseat. Then he ran off toward the school by himself.

This isn't happening, I thought as I sat there waiting for Danny to come back. This can't be happening to me.

Danny returned a few minutes later. He was pretty proud of himself. "Just wait'll everybody sees it," he said, laughing. "This'll really shake them up."

All I wanted was for the nightmare to end, to figure out some way to get home. "Tina," I said sharply, "Tina!" Finally she woke up. "Tell me how to get to Mark's house," I ordered. "We'll drop him off and then go to your house. Then you can get a car and follow me to Danny's and then you can drive me home. All right?"

"Okay," she said groggily. "I guess."

"Wow," Danny said in drunken admiration. "Jenny's just like a general, you know? The way she maps out the strategy and gives the orders and stuff? Wow."

Yeah, just like a general, all right, that's me, I thought sarcastically. Always in charge. What am I going to do? What am I going to do? I thought desperately. Just get home. Just do it, a calm voice inside me said. Worry about the rest later.

Everyone was really quiet on the way to Mark's house, even Danny. I usually hate driving at night because you have to concentrate so hard and adjust the headlights all the time just to make sure you can see the road, but that night it was like I was doing everything automatically, like my arms and legs knew what to do on their own.

Memories flashed through my brain of all the times I'd fallen asleep on the backseat of our car while my mom or dad drove through the night, and suddenly I felt more grown-up, more responsible than I'd ever felt before, because everyone was counting on me. I wished for a second that I could be a kid in the backseat again, and then I turned the wheel slightly to avoid an oncoming car.

Suddenly Tina was leaning up against the front seat and pointing out the window. "Make a left here, Jenny," she said, sounding wide-awake. "Mark's driveway is right there by the third mailbox."

Mark stumbled out of the car and Tina stayed leaning against the seat, giving me directions to her house. Danny had fallen asleep, thank goodness, and in between Tina's directions it was very quiet because I wasn't saying anything back except "okay" or "right" or "uh-huh." I could feel Tina staring out the windshield over my shoulder, and it was kind of peaceful in a way to know that she was there, awake and paying attention too, that I wasn't totally on my own anymore.

"Jenny," she said after a long silence, "I'm really sorry. I really am. I just didn't know what else to do."

"I know," I answered, and I almost added automatically, "It's all right," but I couldn't quite get the words out.

When we got to Tina's house, she said, "I'll have to run in the house for a minute and tell my parents I need the car. I'll try not to take too long."

I nodded okay, but the truth was I couldn't stand the idea of being alone in the car with Danny. For the first minute or so that Tina was gone, I stared out the window and tried to ignore him. But as the time dragged on—what was she doing in there?—I couldn't resist looking at him.

I've never been so angry at anybody in my whole life as I was at Danny at that moment. I wanted to scream at him or punch him or . . . something. But I knew that wouldn't do any good. The only way out of this mess was to stay as quiet and calm as possible. So I stared out the window again, willing Tina to pop out the front door.

Finally she did, dangling the car keys in front of her. I noticed she had a sweatshirt on now, which her parents had probably made her put on. That's probably what took so long, I decided. I backed out of the driveway to let Tina out and then followed her to Danny's.

All the way to his house, I kept trying to pretend he wasn't there beside me. I tried to convince myself I was all alone, just taking a drive. It didn't work, but it kept my mind busy at least.

Then came the worst part of the night, when I had to park Danny's car in the driveway and wake him up. I knew I was finally going to break down and cry the second I had to turn and face him. I was afraid to touch him, afraid for him to wake up again. It was so peaceful with him asleep. And I was afraid to call his name because I knew I'd start crying or yelling or both at once.

When Tina showed up at the car window, I handed her Danny's keys and told her to keep them till the next day. Then I told her I'd wait in her car while she got Danny up and into the house. "Tell him I went home," I whispered. "He'll believe you."

By the time Tina opened the door of her car and sat down next to me, I was half asleep and didn't say a word. I knew she knew the way to my house and I was tired of being in charge, of deciding things. I was so exhausted.

The next thing I knew Tina was shaking me gently and saying, "Wake up, Jenny, we're here."

"Oh, thanks," I said groggily. "Good night." My house has never looked so good as it did that night as I struggled up the driveway, in the front door, and up to bed.

I was actually asleep by the time by parents got home, and I didn't wake up till my mother yelled upstairs to me on her way out the door the next morning. I felt very tired and my body felt incredibly heavy as I rolled out of bed. But I didn't remember why I felt so bad until I looked at myself in the mirror. Oh no, I thought, with a sickening feeling. It wasn't a nightmare. It was real. What was I going to do?

The dread I felt as I walked to school was pretty awful, but nothing could prepare me for actually seeing the school building. The high school is made of white brick, and Danny had written things all over the front of it in huge red letters. Dirty things about the principal. And about Ms. Rafferty. When I saw that, I felt like I was going to throw up, except there was nothing in my stomach. Everyone was rushing up to the school and talking in excited voices. But I felt like I was made of lead, like I could barely move.

I walked through that day in a trance. In home room I heard the buzz of excited conversation, and I heard the principal make an announcement about school pride and self-respect and the guilty coming forward. Afterward I noticed that Danny wasn't in school that day, but Mark and Tina were. Tina and I passed each other in the hall, but neither of us could look the other in the eye. Everybody was talking about the graffiti all day long. A few kids thought it was funny, but most considered it pretty gross. I remember Amy saying at lunch that whoever had done it should be expelled. Sometimes I felt very scared. And sometimes it all seemed totally unreal.

During study hall, I asked for a pass to return the SAT book to Mrs. Rubins, the guidance counselor. I'd carried the book back and forth from school a few times but never looked at it. It had sat in my locker for days now.

That's not really why I went to see Mrs. Rubins, though. I guess somewhere in my mind I knew that even then. But it still surprised me when I found myself talking to her about the graffiti.

"Feel prepared now, Jenny?" she asked with enthusiasm when I handed her the book.

"Kind of," I said halfheartedly.

"Anything else I can do? Any questions?" she continued, but I could tell she wanted to get back to the papers on her desk.

"No, that's okay," I said, smiling weakly as I backed out the door. But I popped my head back into her office a few seconds later, and the tears were starting to escape by then. "Can I talk to you, Mrs. Rubins?" I asked.

She looked up, saw it was serious, and got up and closed the door. "Sure, that's what I'm here for. Have a seat," she said kindly. Then she sat back at her desk and asked, "What's up?"

It took me awhile to get it out because every time I started to say "I know who did the graffiti," I got all choked up and my chest started heaving, and I couldn't do it.

"I know . . ." I took a deep breath and closed my eyes, and some tears were squeezed out. I started again. "I know . . . about the graffiti. I was there when it happened."

There was silence for a few seconds, and when I looked up at Mrs. Rubins, I could tell she was surprised.

"I see," she said, stalling for time.

"And I don't know what to do," I continued. "I can't stand knowing the truth about who did it, but I don't know what to do."

"What do you *want* to do about it?" she said. Her eyes were sympathetic, but she spoke very matter-of-factly.

"What would you *like* to do about it?" Mrs. Rubins repeated.

"But it's not up to me . . . is it?" I asked in confusion.

"Isn't it?" she said, gently but firmly. "You're

really the only one who can decide, Jenny." she paused a minute. "And since you've come in here to talk about it, that probably means you want to tell someone what happened, right?"

"Well . . . maybe I could tell you," I said. "But then . . . you'd have to tell the principal, wouldn't you? And then I'd be betraying someone . . . a friend." I paused. "And I feel maybe, in a way, it was sort of my fault."

"How could it be your fault?" Mrs. Rubins said. "Was it your idea? Did you hand this person the spray paint? Did you tell him . . . or her to do it?"

"No!" I protested. "I'd never do any of those things."

"Then how can it be your fault, Jenny?" she asked again.

I sighed. "Well, I think this person probably did this because of me . . . because he was angry and hurt . . . and I don't know, maybe if I hadn't said certain things or done certain things, this never would have happened."

Mrs. Rubins took off her glasses and rubbed her eyes. It was Friday afternoon and she looked exhausted. "Here's something you need to know: no one is really responsible for what someone else decides to do. It's hard enough being responsible for yourself, right?"

"I guess," I said, still not so sure.

"Look," she said, "Tell you what, why don't you go home and think this over, and we'll talk on Monday. I'll write you a pass. There's no point in going to the principal's office now anyway, because I happen to know that Mr. Bellman's leaving early to go away for the weekend, so he doesn't want to deal with all this right now anyway. Go home. Think it over. Maybe you can convince this person to come forward on his own."

I shrugged. "Okay." It was a relief being spared going to the principal's office. But I felt like I'd go crazy thinking about this all weekend. And Mrs. Rubins didn't seem to understand at all what I meant about being responsible.

She wrote the pass and then looked up. "And don't worry. You're going to get through this, I promise."

That was easy for her to say, I thought.

Everything I passed on the way home looked so strange to me, kind of quaint and innocent. My problem made me feel like an outsider to all the everyday, normal things like people buying slices of pizza or pushing baby carriages. Having a big problem made all the little ones seem totally unimportant. Homework and SATs and Amy seemed very far away.

I went home and went to sleep the way Mrs. Rubins had suggested. When the phone rang, it woke me out of a deep, deep sleep. It must have rung twenty times before I finally picked it up.

"Hello?" I said groggily, turning the word into a question.

"Jenny, it's me. Are you all right?" It was Amy, sounding very worried.

"Oh . . . Hi, Amy. I'm okay."

"I just wanted to tell you that I don't believe you did it. I'm sure it's all that jerk Danny's fault."

"Did what?" I asked in amazement, wondering how she could possibly know. Had Mrs. Rubins lied about not going to the principal right away?

"Everybody knows about the graffiti, Jenny. Some kids found a tiny heart at the bottom of all the writing. It had the initials D.O. and J.G. in it—Danny Ondich and Jenny Gallagher. That plus the stuff about Ms. Rafferty—who gave Danny detention last week, right?—didn't make it too hard to figure out who had done it. Anyway, the principal knows about it too now."

She paused. "How come you don't know about all this? I thought that's why they sent you home. Everybody in school is saying the two of you did it together, but I don't believe it."

She paused again. "You didn't, did you?"

"No," I sighed. "But I was there."

"You were?" Amy said in surprise. "Oh. But that doesn't mean you're really a part of it . . . does it?"

"I don't know, Amy. I'm awfully tired. I think I have to hang up now."

"Okay . . . Hey, Jenny? I'm sorry. I mean, I'm sorry this had to happen to you."

"Yeah. Me too. Thanks . . . thanks for believing in me."

"Call me anytime you want to talk, Jen, okay? I'll be here. Really. I mean it."

"Thanks, Ame. I have to sleep now." And I hung up the phone and collapsed on the bed. It's over, I thought in relief as I drifted off. Everybody knows now, so it's all over.

When I woke up, my parents were already home, fixing chili for dinner.

"Well, hello," Mom said cheerfully as I walked into the kitchen. "You must have had a hard week. I poked my head into your room when I got home, and you were sound asleep."

"I think I know just how you feel," Dad said.

looking up from chopping onions. "I had a real killer week too."

I sat down at the kitchen table watching them for a few minutes, knowing as soon as I opened my mouth and told them what was going on, everything was going to change. Mom was humming a happy song, and everything seemed so calm and peaceful right then. It's weird how boring, everyday things seem to stand out when you have a problem.

"I have to talk to you about something," I suddenly said, plunging right in.

"What?" they both said at the same time, looking up from their work.

"I'm sort of in trouble," I said.

"Oh, Jenny, oh no," Mom said, fearing the worst.

"It's not really bad," I added. "I'm just sort of in the middle of something."

"Does this have something to do with Danny?" Dad asked, looking me right in the eye.

I looked down at the table and nodded. And then I started to cry.

"Okay, Jen, okay," Mom said, putting her hand on mine. "Just tell us everything. Whatever it is, we can handle it."

So I told them everything that had happened the night before, including the part about feeling like it was sort of my fault.

"That's ridiculous," Mom said as soon as I said that. "I'm not saying you're a saint, but you can't feel guilty for something you didn't do."

"Have you talked to Danny about this today, Jen?" Dad asked. "Do you know what he plans to do about it?"

"No, but I'm sure they'll call us both into the principal's office on Monday. Besides, I don't really want to talk to him. I'm sort of afraid . . . or embarrassed, I guess."

Mom sighed. "Well, it seems to me all you can do is tell the truth and hope Danny does the same," she said. "In the meantime, there's no use worrying about it. I know you can't help it, but it won't do any good, believe me. Your father and I have to get this chili started, so why don't you take the car and go pick up some nacho chips and bean dip, okay?"

"Okay," I answered in a daze. I was still waiting for them to start yelling at me, to tell me what a failure I was as a daughter, and how I couldn't ever see Danny again. But they weren't doing that. They were acting so calm. What was going on?

While I was driving to the store, I figured it out. They wanted to get me out of the house so they could have a talk and figure out what to do next, how to "handle" me. There was more to come. I was sure of it.

After a pretty silent dinner, Dad went out to the garage to look for some old magazines he kept out there, and Mom and I did the dishes. We were pretty quiet the whole time, until I was drying the last dish.

"Jenny," she finally said, sounding like she'd been thinking something over a long time. "What do you think is going to happen between you and Danny now, once this spray-paint situation is all over, I mean? Have you thought about that?"

"I don't really know," I said, bracing myself for her to announce another "lesson" I'd learned.

"Well, you know, you are two very different kinds of people, and that can make it tough on a relationship."

I'd been ready to reject anything she told me, but what she'd just said was hard to deny.

"Sometimes," I admitted. "But sometimes it makes it kind of interesting, kind of exciting, to be with someone so different."

She smiled. "I know people who've been in relationships like that. Not your father and me. I mean, he may have been kind of on the wild side at one time, but deep down we always had the same values, really. But I've had friends who've been in your situation. It's not easy, is it?"

"No," I agreed, feeling like I was being taken seriously for once because Mom was comparing me to her adult friends. "What happened to them? I mean the people you knew?" I asked.

She sighed. "Oh, different things. Sometimes it worked out and sometimes it didn't. Sometimes it worked for a while, until one person or both people realized how unhappy they really were." She thought a minute. "The bad part is when people are so different, have such different values, I mean, that they hurt each other just by being themselves, you know? Because then neither of them can win as long as they're together."

"Oh," I said, feeling like I'd just been kicked in the stomach, because that description seemed to fit Danny and me perfectly, and I didn't want to believe it or let Mom see how much it affected me. I hung up the dish towel, letting Mom know I'd done enough talking for one night. I gave her a quick kiss on the cheek. "I

have to get started on my geometry homework.
I'm way behind. And then I'll probably just go
to bed, okay?"

"Okay, honey," she said sadly, like she was
accepting for the first time that there really
wasn't anything she could do for me, that I had
to do it myself. "Sleep tight," she called out.

They called Danny and me to the principal's
office first thing on Monday, and when I got
there, Danny was already waiting outside. We
hadn't talked at all since Thursday night.

"Hi," he said, looking up quickly and then
staring at his feet.

"Hi," I said, sitting down next to him.

"Let's leave Mark and Tina out of this, okay?"
he said.

I thought about it. "I don't know if I can," I
said honestly. "I mean, I just want to tell the
whole story and get this over with. If I try to
make things up or leave things out, I'll just get
confused."

"Okay. Never mind." He looked over at me.
"What's *your* problem? You look like you're going
to the electric chair or something. You didn't
do anything, so what do you have to worry
about?"

"I thought maybe you blamed me or something . . . for what happened."

"Why?" he said, not really knowing what I
meant. "What did you do?"

I just shrugged my shoulders and looked away,
not knowing what to say, how to explain it.

They called Danny in first, and I had to wait
outside. They probably want to see if our stories match I decided, feeling like a criminal in a
detective show.

The principal was pretty nice to me when it was my turn, so Danny must have taken all the blame. Before I left, though, he shook his head and said, "How did a nice young lady like you get mixed up with a kid like that?"

I didn't say anything. I didn't think he had any right to ask me that, but he was the principal, so there wasn't anything I could do about it.

Danny was waiting for me right outside the office.

"Thanks," I said when I saw him.

"For what?" he asked.

"For not getting me in trouble," I answered.

"Why would I do that? God, you must think I'm really a jerk." And he walked away.

Danny was suspended for two weeks after that, and I didn't see him or talk to him all that time until the Saturday before he was supposed to come back to school. He called me up and asked me if I wanted to go to some stock-car races with him. It wasn't my idea of a dream date, but I said okay.

My parents were very polite when he came to pick me up, but I knew they were worried, wondering whether it was starting up all over again.

I think I knew as soon as I saw Danny that day that there wasn't anything to worry about. It was like I saw for the first time how different we really were, how everything that had ever happened to either of us was pulling us away from each other, off into the different directions we had to go.

The races were really noisy, so we couldn't talk much, and the cars roaring around the track didn't interest me much, so I ended up daydreaming a lot, thinking about things I'd put off for a while, since I'd known Danny, really. Stuff like colleges and moving up a seat in orchestra, and planning a surprise party for Amy's birthday in November. I suddenly missed Amy a whole lot, like I'd been away on a long trip or something.

Danny wanted to get a burger after the races, but I made some excuse and said I couldn't. When we pulled up in front of my house, he gave me a quick kiss, like we were going to see each other again soon, and I felt like I was being torn apart inside. I had to say something, now, before I lost my nerve and got back into making the same old mistakes.

"Danny," I said, with my hand on the door handle, "I think maybe . . . we should start going out with other people. Don't you?"

It was like he'd sort of been expecting it. "Okay, sure," he said coldly. "Good-bye."

I tried to explain. "It's not just because of what happened . . ." I started.

"Sure. I know," he said, cutting me off. "Nice knowing you, Jenny."

"Danny, please don't, please?"

"Bye, Jenny," he said, staring straight ahead.

I got out of the car, and he took off the second the door slammed shut.

I went up to my room and tried to start writing out note cards for a term paper in English, but tears kept falling on the cards and blurring the ink.

Right before dinner, I heard my mother call upstairs, "Jenny, Amy's here. I'm sending her up."

"Hi, Jen," she said, walking into my room.

"Hi, Amy," I said. "How's it going?"

"Okay. How about you?"

It wasn't a very exciting conversation, but it felt pretty good. We talked about school awhile, and then Amy was quiet for a few minutes.

"This is kind of embarrassing," she said, reaching into the back pocket of her jeans, "but I wanted to give you something. This," she said, handing me a folded magazine article.

"What is it?" I said, starting to open it up.

"No, don't!" she said. "Wait till I leave, okay?"

"Why?"

"You might be mad at me when you see what it is," she explained. "But I just read this, and I thought of you. Read it after I leave, but first promise that you won't hate me, okay?"

"Amy!" I shrieked. "Why would I hate you? What is this?" I started opening it up again.

"Don't! Wait till I leave. And say you promise!"

"Okay, okay, I promise," I said, giving in and tossing the article onto my desk. Then we stared at each other in silence for a while. "So what's new?" I finally said.

We talked a little bit, but we were both nervous, and Amy left a few minutes later. Somehow I knew the article would have something to do with Danny, and it did. It was from one of the teen magazines Amy always read. She said she bought them just to look at the ads for clothes, but I'd always suspected she read them from cover to cover, especially the articles that gave advice. She just didn't like to admit she needed any, that's all.

The article was called "Are You in Love with Mr. Wrong?" Oh no, I thought. I don't need this. Not now. But I couldn't help being curious, so I started reading it. There were lots of true stories in it about girls who fell for boys who were really different just because they were curious and wanted to rebel against their families. This isn't about me, I said to myself, but I kept on reading.

The part that really got to me said that some girls like boys they feel sorry for or feel better than because that gives them an excuse to avoid their own problems. It said that reforming your boyfriend was really an excuse for not living up to your own potential. "That's crazy," I said out loud, and threw the article across the room.

Danny didn't call me again; I'm not sure he ever looked at me again, not really. Every once in a while when we would pass each other in the halls at school, I'd feel my heart pound and my face go red. But Danny just looked right through me as if we'd never met or kissed or held each other.

It scared me to think how close I'd come to being part of Danny's life, going along in Danny's direction and forgetting about my own. It had seemed so easy in a way, like I could just drift along. But that was all over. I couldn't go back to that feeling if I tried. I was back to the same old problems, the same old worries.

Was I ever going to figure myself out—figure out where I was going and what side I was on? Would I ever fall in love again? And would it end up the same way if I did?

For a long time, I went through the motions of my pre-Danny life—studying, going to games, trying to get back to my old friends.

I'm still going through the motions of having

the life I had before Danny, but it's getting a little easier. I still don't find most of the boys in my school very interesting. And I still think Danny had something exciting that most of them don't have. But I'm trying not to worry so much about boys and taking sides and all that stuff for a while. Any day now, I expect my life will start to fit again, to feel right.

Everybody says that girls just grow up faster than boys and you just have to wait for them to catch up.

I'm waiting.